YOUR MIND IS A TERRIBLE THING

A novella by Hailey Piper

Layout of the M.G. Yellowjacket, Crossing F009333A

Pod A: Bridge
Pod B: Quarters 1
Pod C: Processing, Supplementary Core
Pod D: Water Treatment 1
Pod E: Main Shuttle Access
Pod F: Storage 1
Pod G: Kitchen/Dining
Pod H: Physical Recreation
Pod I: Shuttle Parts Storage
Pod J: Wraith Repair Center
Pod K: Cargo Hold 1
Pod L: Cargo Hold 2
Pod M: Accounts
Pod N: Crew Lounge
Pod O: Water Treatment 2
Pod P: Quarters 2
Pod Q: Quarters 3
Pod R: Storage 2
Pod S: Cargo 3
Pod T: Cargo 4

Table of Contents

MIND-HACK

1

The brain was to blame. Simple as that.

Inner snow flew from the bad side of Alto's brain, as if their mind belonged to someone else. Personal wants and needs were junk against a head full of bizarre chemical imbalances and a cruel bias against having a good time.

They watched Esme explore the bedroom, cream walls and dark tile floor giving little more space than a walk-in closet by terrestrial standards. Every inch mattered on a starship.

But Esme's room had to be larger, right? That couldn't matter; no need to compare the quarters of a counselor versus a comms specialist. And either way, Esme was here. After a nice meal and conversation in Pod G's kitchen, she had followed to Alto's room and shed her coat and boots, which meant she wanted to stay.

Why the hell couldn't Alto enjoy the moment? This rocketing pitter-patter heartrate echoed schooltime crushes of yesteryear. The worst classes could be brightened so long as your eye-candy idol showed up that day.

Esme was better than any teenage fantasy. She was thirty-eight, and gorgeous and round and confident, and her violet eyes shined brighter than any star. Black hair hung loose to either side of her rosy face and past her shoulders. She wore a button-up short-sleeved crimson blouse and slacks as white as her shed coat. Bare feet padded Alto's room, Esme's toenails painted the same dark purple as her fingernails. Self-assured in every way, like the room belonged to her. She spread a grabby hand and plucked up a small instrument from one of several wall cubbies filled with trinkets and scrap-paper memories beside Alto's bed.

"A harmonica," Esme said, her voice dry and soothing. "You play?"

Alto shrank to insignificance under that violet gaze, nothing but a stick-like insect with chopped-down bright blue hair, the kind to mistakenly crawl onto a starship. Once upon a time, intrusive thoughts had told Alto no one liked them, everyone was pretending. Sometimes riding those thoughts had brought relief. If no one cared, why should Alto?

Esme crushed those illusions under word and heel, both through sessions and her genuine compassion. She cared, and somehow that made Alto's inner snow fall heavier. Now there were good moments Alto risked losing if they twisted into knots and forgot how to be a person in this room, with this woman.

"Play," Alto echoed. Their hands were shaking as if someone had shut off heat to the Pod Q living quarters. "Strong word, but solitary hobbies help when you travel cross-planet ships so often."

Let alone aboard a corpse ship, but Alto kept that nervous detail tucked behind their lips. A reminder of the M.G. Yellowjacket's cargo might kill the mood.

Esme tossed the harmonica to Alto and nodded at them. "Play for me."

The command stirred Alto into an apprehensive smile. They tapped at the harmonica's synth-wood comb, raised the brass reed plates to their lips, and out came a nameless tune of slow notes and long sighs.

Esme listened without watching, as if she knew her gaze might shake nerves and knock planets from orbit. The music seemed to settle her with the air. She belonged in this room, taken by the harmonica's charms, and Alto couldn't be sure if they were savoring this moment or stalling the next. When the nameless song felt finished, they tossed the harmonica back.

"Beautiful," Esme said. She hummed to herself and then placed the harmonica into its cubby. "I've heard the music while passing through the lounge up-ship, but I never knew it was you. I'm surprised you never mentioned it during sessions. For coping, I mean."

Alto wanted to say something playful, but their brain

wondered if they were a liar by omission. Esme was right. Not once in therapy sessions had Alto noted the harmonica, or the entertainment wraith they kept in their quarters closet, or how beautiful they found Esme.

The room's chill deepened under another bout of inner snow. Alto hadn't weighed whether a counselor/client date was appropriate, and now they'd taken the step of inviting Esme to the room, and her coat and boots lay beside the sliding door, and the bad side of Alto's brain asked, *Could Esme lose her job for this?* Alto had been seeing Esme for sessions through the past two crossings. Granted, everyone aboard any starship suffered some form of anxiety or depression, especially the crew of a corpse ship. How could casual conversation fight the knowledge that the dead filled four cargo holds?

Sometimes therapy felt pointless.

Except Esme had taught Alto that their brain was to blame, not themselves, whatever that distinction meant. Brains were organs like hearts and kidneys, and likewise they could malfunction, rough as any comm unit under Alto's repair. If Esme lost her job, there would be no more sessions with anyone. Another Perfect Alto Fuck-Up, this time ruining someone else's life on the way down.

"Will this be okay?" Alto asked. They should have thought of these complications sooner, but they'd been too captivated by confidence and beauty and brilliant eyes.

Esme turned from the wall, and a new atmosphere breathed from her posture. No more curiosity and concern. A wild heat burned in her skin, and she approached Alto with deliberate steps, the ceiling light sliding down her curves.

Alto's chest turned heavy. They wanted to let this moment happen, but their conscience fought the trembling desire inside. Or was that anxious snow making excuses against a moment's happiness? If only the human head weren't so complicated.

"I don't want to get you breaking ethics, that's all," Alto said, voice rising in pitch. "As my therapist, you know?"

"Oh Alto," Esme said, almost a purr. "I'm not like other therapists. I'm a fun therapist."

Alto's thoughts squirmed again, doubting every moment in one last-ditch attempt at sabotaging this sweet visit. Why would Esme want Alto, this wiry jittery nonsense mess who couldn't make their own brain shut up for a few hours?

Words spilled out before Alto could stop. "Don't want to get you in trouble," they said, clambering backward onto the bed.

"You won't," Esme said.

She climbed onto the bed's foot. Blouse buttons hung loose from their catches, leaving fabric flaps dangling, and the light chased the curves of her breasts and belly. Every covering fell away the closer she came.

Alto slid toward the headboard, told the lights to dim, and slipped inch by inch from their black pants, white tank, everything. Clothes sometimes seemed like material shame, a way to cover Alto at their best. As they shed, the inner snow thinned. No crystal fragments flying inside the mind, only clear weather of a rare kind.

Alto's asking turned playful. "Sure you won't get in trouble?" they asked with half a smirk.

"You're worried," Esme said, pausing midway up Alto's chest. "Do you still want this?"

Alto let the word burst out: "Yes."

"That's all that matters."

Esme planted a soft kiss on collarbone, neck, beneath jaw. Excited nerves rippled down Alto's body, where flesh and metal fused between their legs. A thought could change this fusion's shape.

Esme's fingers brushed Alto's inner thigh. "You never mentioned this, either."

"A surprise," Alto whispered.

Below their waist, the augmentation of tissue and machine either allowed their natural hollow space to open and shut, or to swell into a mountain. In, out, anything between.

"Whatever you like, I can do," Alto said. "Best time for everyone. A good surprise?"

"I like your surprises." Esme ran a hand down Alto's chest, between the slanted scars beneath each dark nipple. "I like you."

"Likewise." Alto raised a cautious hand. "That's why I don't want trouble for you."

"Alto," Esme scolded.

"You're the best thing on this ship," Alto said, now in

full smirk. "And I'd hate to—"

"Alto." Esme's whisper was bouncy yet stern.

She pressed down, and Alto held her close, not another word between them, only laughter and sighs and a tender space between their skins, where anxiety found a quick death.

Esme managed to stagger to the bathroom and back, Alto after her, and then they both clung naked on the bed, where abstract dreams swirled through Alto's head. Everyone else talked about their dreams like stories, but Alto only knew shapes and colors, scents and sounds and the illusion of touch. At the dreamscape's edge, fingertips stroked their naked back, and purple paint coated their sensations.

Esme again. She wanted closeness, and Alto's skin tingled with mutual hunger. Alto had known their share of rough experiences, either with women who changed their minds at seeing the augmentation or those who treated a designer mecha-vulva/cock combo like coming face-to-face with their souls. Esme was different, self-assured, and she recognized the human mixed with the machine. Alto rolled over and opened eager eyes.

The bed was empty.

Alto sat up. "Esme?"

A hollow space in the tangled sheets showed where Esme used to lie. Shadows coated the bed's surroundings, but the dim room hid no one. There was nowhere to disappear, and no light shined beside the shut bathroom door to suggest it was occupied.

She had left. The augmentation wasn't a problem, but while Alto had tasted sugar on eager lips, for Esme the sex must have been terrible, some new regret on her dance card, and a woman so lovely likely kept a long one. She had waited out of politeness for Alto to fall asleep before leaving.

"Stop," Alto said, tapping their forehead. Palm struck skin, and an answering tap echoed from the hall. "Esme?"

Her boots and coat remained beside the shut bedroom door. Alto saw no other clothes, but Esme might not have left, only gotten lost in the dark in search of the bathroom and wandered into the hall by accident.

Alto slid from the bed, bare feet filling with the floor's cold. Checking the hall naked didn't bother them, but someone else would find it inappropriate. Alto had no robe and getting dressed felt like abandoning future closeness with Esme when they found her, so they drew a sheet from the bed, wrapped it around their torso, and slipped into the hall.

Pod Q's dim corridor curved in a ring, its outer circular wall punctuated by shut sliding doors to the slender airlock, four bedrooms, and the exits to Pod P and Pod R. Amber lights dotted the ceiling, their glow catching a shape lying on the dark floor.

Someone had collapsed outside Alto's bedroom.

Panic flashed in snow squalls through their head until squatting close revealed this was not Esme. Too narrow. Too many pieces scattered along Pod Q's inner circle, as if someone had smashed a glass the size of a person.

16

Pod Q's service wraith lay inches from Alto's toes. Once a living person, and then a dormant corpse, some Merchant Guild facility had later processed it into a calcified husk and fitted cybernetics across its body. In normal circumstances, a black shell of a mask hid the skull face beneath psionic wraith-nodes and an interface display. A segmented brace-like wraith-plate usually clung to the torso and fused around the spine. This joined the pelvis in forming a snakish tail, easier than legs for the wraith to slide through the small cylindrical wraith-ports that connected starship pods.

All that complicated fusion lay strewn outside Alto's room. The wraith's spine and tail fizzed and twitched where wires curled between spiny vertebrae. The wraith-plate stretched from sternum and pelvis, leaving no support for the body. A heavy blow had cracked open the wraith's mask, leaving its nodes to dangle like blinking fruit from a vine. One black socket peered through the shattered darkness, a glimpse of the wraith's skull.

Alto stroked the mask, but no interface lit the display. Out of commission. Somehow even the dead could die again.

The wraith-nodes looked undamaged. Had the wraith sent a psionic cry for help to Grid, the Yellowjacket's A.I.? Would a machine even understand that level of self-preservation? Doubtful one would harm itself by running against the walls, and even then it would have made such a racket as to wake everyone in Pod Q. This damage was deliberate. But who would hurt a wraith? They were defenseless. Core to their design.

Soft skin brushed the floor somewhere down the hall. Alto pivoted on their heels, still squatting, about to open their mouth and ask again for Esme.

Their breath caught in a choked gasp.

The ceiling lights reflected in the glistening surface of a nest of maroon snakes. They writhed against the walls and floor, growing out from a dark lump hidden in the gloom. Their heads whipped toward Alto—no, not snakes. These were hollow tubes, as if someone's intestines had been torn out, cut into pieces, and given new life.

Alto slid back on one heel and thrashed one protective hand outward. Their choked gasp broke into a squeaking cry as a purple-lit curtain of pain fell over their eyes.

Pod Q shrank to a bruise-colored hallway and filled with silhouetted figures dashing in a furious circle. They were people, and they weren't people, and Alto couldn't tell why or how that made any sense. One shape swerved from the pack and slammed into Alto's chest, knocking them off-balance.

Their back struck Pod Q's cold floor, their sheet flopped over their body, and the purple curtain parted from the dim hall.

"What—" Alto started, but their voice caught in another gasp.

The tubes slapped up Alto's legs, over the sheet, across their pelvis. The augmentation shut between their legs almost on reflex, terrified these tubes might try to

18

crawl inside. Beyond their feet, the dark lump at the tubes' root slid into clearer light, and at last a sharp scream rocketed up Alto's throat.

Wrinkled pink-gray flesh curled into a great pulsating brain as large as Alto's chest. Crimson ichor dripped from its underside where it balanced on the snaking tubes, and thick drops spotted the floor with tiny red puddles. A quake rippled down its limbs, spattering the sheet with slime and sending the tubes coiling and digging at Alto's skin.

Alto thrashed their hands to either side. Fingers fell on the shattered wraith's broken mask, and Alto plucked it up as a makeshift bludgeon.

But the wraith had been smashed too hard against the floor. Its mask collapsed around crumbling bone as Alto swung forward, and they only raised a dangling wire of nodes against the feral brain and its furious limbs.

The brain's front wrinkles flexed with bicep-like tension, and a shockwave of purple light filled the hallway.

Alto plummeted down a dim maroon chasm. Wind rushed through their choppy hair and swatted their eyes to tears. They rushed toward some surface, about to splatter meat and bone across an unforgiving floor, they were going to die—

Except Alto wasn't falling, wasn't here. The Yellowjacket had not cracked open over a steel canyon. Some violent thought had driven this purple vision into Alto's mind. Even the airy swirl in their ears carried a false hum, and it somehow sounded purple, too.

The vision's ground flew at Alto's face, and they flinched back into the real hallway of Pod Q, where the brain hovered over Alto's chest, its tubes lashing at neck, face, eyes. Alto thrust their hand over their face, needed to stop this, couldn't let the brain dig inside.

An electronic *ping* rang through Alto's face. They had forgotten that their fist still clutched the wire of nodes. Had the wraith come back online? Could it function enough that a cry for help would spread through the ship?

Another scream tore up Alto's throat as an icicle of wire jammed into their forehead. Starships tended to be cold, but Alto had never felt this frigid intrusion drill through their skin, muscle, skull, seeking and finding their nerves and thoughts, as if Alto's mind were a physical organ to be torn open and catalogued.

And the violent brain was here, too. It grasped at the floor on twisting tubes and lurched toward eyes, brain, and thought. It wanted in.

Alto screamed one last time. The freezing pain cut forward from their skull, as if they'd grown a unicorn horn of ice. Flashing violet rippled down the hallway, across wraith parts and writhing tubes, into the oncoming brain.

The new vision stretched away from Alto, as if they were watching it on a screen rather than being thrust into dreaming it. The walls to either side of the brain spread into a cracked-open starship, its only pod gutted into one vast steely amphitheater housing a violet-tinged cathedral of gore. Shattered bones formed its structure, and flayed corpses dressed its skin. The sight should have iced Alto's blood.

But Alto had suffered the worst chill in their life moments ago, and this pretend idea couldn't freeze them up. It belonged to them, a prize from inside the brain, and they drove the vision sword-like, thought against thought, numb purple failing beneath Alto's sharp violet.

The illusory cathedral tore away, revealing Pod Q's hallway. Red patterns stained Alto's sheet, but neither tubes nor brain dripped new puddles onto over the cloth.

Down the hall, shuddering limbs carried the huge brain away. Thicker slime now dribbled from its underside, and black fluid rotted across its frontal lobe before its dark lump squeezed through a hole in the wall—a floor-level wraith-port. A thumping echo said the brain traveled the channels between ports now, maybe seeking another wraith to destroy. It could wind up on any pod of the Yellowjacket through there, but at least it had gone from here.

Alto sat up shaking. The sheet flopped from their naked chest, and they threw it off and patted down their skin, searching for anything unsavory the feral brain might have left behind.

Only scrapes here, or indent marks there where tubes had coiled around a bare ankle. Nothing but lingering traces. Everything should have been fine.

Except Esme was still missing. Bigger than that, Alto had screamed several times, and no one had answered.

Anxious needles pricked their spine, and their breath charged in and out. They had survived the creature.

Had anyone else?

2

Alto pounded their fist twice against the wall. "Anyone here?" Hollow collisions answered through the pod's cold dim hall, but no voices.

Time ran strange on a starship, stranger with a corpse ship's skeleton crew. Without planetary rotation to designate day and night, the Yellowjacket's eight crewmates kept odd hours from each other, and even then some of them came from worlds with longer periods of light or darkness. Combine rotating shifts with contrasting bodily temperaments, and rarely were two crewmates together, but someone was always awake.

Alto supposed they might be that someone now. Anyone dozing in their rooms could have ignored the brain's tumble through the wraith-port, assuming a wraith on the go.

But crewmates wouldn't have ignored the screams.

Best to hope they had gathered at the lounge in Pod N, or even the meeting room behind the Bridge in Pod A, forgetting Alto along the way for some reason.

Better than the alternative. The Yellowjacket held too many corpses in its cargo holds to assume death on the whole crew. Especially Esme.

Pod Q's lifeless wraith remained at Alto's side. What hope did the living have if even the mechanized dead couldn't catch a break? Alto stroked one tail vertebra, chilly against their fingertips. Being comms specialist did not make them a wraith specialist. This damage was beyond their power to repair.

Built by fusing cybernetics, psionics, and the dead, wraiths worked as avatars for each Merchant Guild ship's A.I., along with any other uses to suit their programming—cleaning, entertainment, you name it. They were cheaper than the living in most roles as far as Merchant Guild was concerned. No feeding, no sleeping, only regular maintenance on their circuitry. Their varied uses and inexpensiveness were reason enough for the Yellowjacket to haul a cargo of corpses which would become wraiths at their destination facility.

The feral brain must have followed this service wraith through the nearby wraith-port and beaten it against the floor until it broke apart. Alto had no idea why. Wraiths were eerie but harmless, and anyone who'd crewed a crossing or two got used to them snaking out of their designated holes in the walls. The wrinkled pink-gray intruder wasn't crew and had probably never encountered a wraith before.

Same as Alto had never heard of anything like this alien across the settled worlds. A large, exposed brain, limbs pouring out its underside instead of a spinal cord, psionic power to attack others' thoughts—sounded like a new discovery had found its way onto the Yellowjacket and hunted this poor wraith with a vengeance.

Alto wrapped the stained sheet around their shoulders and was about to stand when they spotted the glowing dots on the floor. A branching cord of wire had torn from the wraith's mask when Alto had tried to use its head as a weapon. Two ends glowed with wraith-nodes, but another hung frayed where Alto's hand had smashed wire against face.

Their fingers explored eyebrows, temple, forehead—there. A glassy texture ran cool beneath one fingertip.

"That can't be," Alto whispered. They bounded from the broken wraith's side, into their room, dropping their sheet at the door.

The bathroom was a cramped white-metal tube with three tiny cubicles separating toilet, sink, and shower. Bathtubs were not a starship luxury, and Alto had grown used to missing them in lieu of the high-powered recycled hotwash that surged from the shower's ceiling.

Above the sink, a metallic mirror's shiny circle broke up the white wall. Alto's angular sienna face gazed out from the reflection. Their amber eyes shined with stark ceiling light while the skin beneath hung dark with inconsistent sleep. Sweat slicked back their short blue hair from a once-unblemished forehead, where now a teardrop-shaped light glowed above their right eyebrow.

Same place they'd slammed their hand to guard against the brain's tubes. A metal halo circled the dim teardrop, bruising the skin where wires had found purchase and snaked into Alto's tissue and bone.

Their reflection glowed with a psionic wraith-node.

Wraith parts weren't meant for the living. Alto dug their fingernails under the metal rim and curled their hand into a claw. The node had to come out.

A fiery scream split Alto's skull and burst out their mouth, spraying spittle across their reflection. Their free hand thrashed at the sink-mounted ports for toothbrush, mouthwash, quick-acting hair dye. Magnets kept everything in place, much like the node kept rooted in Alto's head.

Strange nerves surged down their body, pricking the spine and swelling the flesh around and within the between-leg augmentation. Skull-splitting pain coiled around bizarre arousal.

These clashing sensations had to be a sign that the node would soon turn lethal, spreading stroke-like misfires through the brain. Alto eased their fingernails between skin and metal. Tried again. Pain in their head. Fuzzy pleasure greasing their augmentation in, out, lighting a pleasant fire through the rest of their body. A thought could shift the flesh-and-metal piece into Alto's natural cavity, or a locked door, or a rising mountain below their waist, the cybernetic wires tracing a route from pelvis, up spine, into brain.

The wraith-node might have wound itself into those same wires when burrowing through Alto's skull. The circuitry had apparently crisscrossed in such a nervous web that their body couldn't distinguish psionics from sexual ebb and flow.

Meaning the augmentation's wires might have saved Alto's life. A freak occurrence, one in a million chance.

Had this ever happened before? Alto had no idea. They weren't an expert in cybernetics, after all, and Jissika, the Yellowjacket's wraith specialist, didn't seem to be hanging around Pod Q to ask. Maintenance tech Elvis might have ideas. He was gone too.

But Alto had another to ask. Not a crewmate, but something more intimately connected to psionic nodes than any human.

They left the bathroom, tangled their feet with the fallen sheet, and stumbled toward the closet on the far side of the bed from the cubby-holed wall. A flat panel door stretched from floor to ceiling, one Alto had made sure to close as they'd led Esme into the room. No need for her to see what lay curled inside the closet. Alto pressed their palm against the panel.

The closet hummed as if pleased by human touch, and its door slid into the wall, revealing a thin dark cylinder where a lump of tangled flesh and circuitry filled the floor.

An intact wraith.

3

Every Merchant Guild ship utilized a network of wraiths to take on the shipboard computer's delegated tasks, and most independent ships purchased at least one for the same purpose. Each Luminous Kingdom starship plugged directly into a living cerebrator, Archon ships fused with genetically engineered fungi, and so on. No one trusted a shipboard A.I. to work alone after the L.K. Cassandra, a tragedy Alto scarcely remembered; it had come and gone when they were still a child. Only a machine would think the right solution to a small shipboard fire was to empty its compartments of air, asphyxiating every living thing.

The wraiths ensured shipboard control's decentralization. If a starship's A.I. got the idea to jettison the air, or set the artificial gravity to ten times E-centric, or shut off heat to every pod, that decision would have to go through the wraiths, and every single undead cyborg would have to malfunction in the same way to carry out the ship-wide massacre. Not impossible, but damn unlikely.

Alto squatted in front of their closet and reached inside. "Wake up, Zelany."

The wraith's flexible metal tail curled in a spiral of inert vertebrae. A wraith-plate clung to the torso like a segmented breastplate for an undead knight. Circuits mapped the arms. A black shell mask coated the skull head, its interface dark but undamaged. In building a wraith, wires followed a corpse's neural and nervous pathways, to Alto's understanding. The pre-laid structure was supposed to be easier than robotics in helping the wraith make intelligent decisions. The dried husk showed no clear indication of gender, ethnicity, anything to tell who they used to be in life, at least to Alto.

Their fingertip touched the mask. Three brow-mounted wraith-nodes flickered to life, and the wraith uncoiled from the floor and slithered from the closet. An electronic start-up jingle played from the mask. Its dark screen switched to an animated sea-green face with oversized white eyes and small antennae sticking up from the head, some artist's idea of a happy cartoon Martian from back when people believed in such things. Alto had chosen this avatar out of thousands, same as Zelany's unique social settings.

"Persons and every-folk!" a boyish electronic voice said. "Welcome to the greatest show from Earth!"

The personality was an ancient archetype, something Alto had stumbled on while playing with the menu. They'd never changed it—Zelany was fun this way—but now Alto wished they remembered how to adjust him back to neutral, at least temporarily. This was a time for straight answers, not goofing around.

Alto unfolded from the floor to their full height of five and a half feet, which put Zelany at chest height when balancing on his tail. Head to final vertebra, he stretched longer than most humans.

"Zelany, I need to be serious right now," Alto said, almost parental.

"You got it, champ," Zelany said, waving his needle-like hands. "No funny business."

Alto rubbed their forehead without thinking and nudged the embedded node. A psionic knife scraped through their head and then branched into confused excitement. They flinched as if touching fire, hand off forehead, and then pointed to the node.

"Will this kill me?" Alto asked.

A white sheen flickered across Zelany's digital face. "A quick scan says you're in audition-ready shape."

Alto almost rubbed their forehead again in frustration but stopped in time. A lone wraith had little chance of figuring out what had happened inside Alto's skull without cracking it open and sifting through the organic hardware. They needed a stronger computer. And they needed to know what had happened to the ship, the crew, the—visitor.

"Never mind my head," Alto said. "Contact Grid for ship status."

Zelany's digital face went placid, and an automated feminine voice overtook his personality setting: *No contact available. Please speak with your shipboard communications specialist.*

Meaning Alto. They almost laughed. "What the hell am I supposed to do?"

Zelany's digital face regained control. "Unprepared for the part?" he asked. "Don't worry, champ, we will read that script and rehearse around the clock."

Alto took Zelany's head into their hands and thumbed through settings until a comms info window popped up. Zelany's cartoon Martian face groaned to one side as if being crushed, but another menu soon covered him, this one running a column of numbers. His communications must have glitched when Alto last shut him down. That was the only explanation.

Except it wasn't. Every number checked out, every connection gave a ready sign, and general readings said Zelany's wraith-nodes were in tip-top condition. His psionic messages read as sent, but Grid did not receive.

Which meant the problem wasn't in the wraith, but in the ship's A.I. core at the Bridge. Had the feral brain slid through the wraith-ports to Pod A and severed crucial wires within Grid's terminal? Wraiths were supposed to keep pests in check, but the brain had shown no problem shattering the Pod Q wraith to pieces.

Grim thoughts slithered down Alto's mind. "Contact

the other wraiths. Tell one of them to check on crew, or Grid, or—anything, I guess."

Zelany's avatar gritted cartoon teeth. "Looks like we're booked for a one-wraith show."

Sometimes when Alto fixated on the digital avatar, they forgot about the body, circuitry, how that face displayed from the mask of an undead cyborg. They moved to check Zelany's systems again, but there was no point. He was perfect. The other wraiths were the problem.

"Nothing?" Alto asked. "Every wraith's out of commission?"

Zelany hummed. "Might've found an understudy."

Alto's hand felt heavy. They glanced down and found a paper brochure between their fingers. Bold letters crossed the purple cover, reading THE WAY OF THE WRAITH, and beneath them danced little wraiths in top hats and suits, their jackets flapping comically over serpentine tails. A benign tinkering in the mind, little more than a psionic raindrop.

Alto let the brochure float away in the artificial gravity. "Quit psionic scan. I'm not a wraith."

The brochure vanished before it hit the floor, and Zelany's tail twitched where it would have landed.

Alto raised a hand to rub their forehead and then remembered and instead ran fingers through blue locks. Best case scenario, the Yellowjacket's other wraiths were on the fritz. Worst case scenario, the violent brain had chased each one through the wraith-ports and smashed them across the ship, with only Zelany spared. The only way to speak with Grid would be a personal trip to Pod A.

Except in an even worse scenario, the brain had also destroyed Grid, and the M.G. Yellowjacket would soon lose its heat, water, gravity, and air. Alto and the rest of the crew wouldn't live long then. Likely the others had gathered at Pod A. Maybe Esme had wandered that way, oblivious to the emergency, with no way to warn Alto now that comms were down.

If everyone wasn't already dead.

"Stop it," Alto whispered.

Their brain would take the situation and run amok if they let it. Keep it simple—was there gravity? Yes. Therefore, the feral brain hadn't destroyed Grid, at least not down to its subsystems. Communications were offline. Nothing else was certain, no need to catastrophize.

Alto sighed toward Zelany's display. "What'd you last hear from Grid before shutdown?"

"Word from the cheap seats," Zelany said, and his cartoon face winked. "Management says we got to receive, got to spread the word."

Merchant Guild protocol only directed that messages overtake all other A.I. functions when there was a corporate directive or a distress call. Zelany probably wouldn't refer to Merchant Guild directors as speaking *from the cheap seats*, which only left some other ship's cry for help.

"Play the message," Alto said.

Zelany's face went placid again, and a bar filled his display's lower half with jagged audio lines. "Captain Afsar Sajid of the Star-Hopper," the audio said, the voice desperate. "Only a handful of us left now, and we need immediate extraction from planet's surface. Please help, anyone." There was a pause and then: "Captain Afsar Sajid of the Star-Hopper."

The message repeated, set to automated loop by the Star-Hopper's captain. Protocol would have forced Grid to replay the entire loop through the Yellowjacket's systems, but Alto made Zelany shut it off at the fourth recitation.

"Which planet?" Alto asked.

Zelany looked puzzled. "Grid didn't jot that in the script notes."

Likely Grid had received the message minutes before Alto had shut Zelany down. Had the Yellowjacket been traveling toward the unnamed planet while Alto and Esme slept? Did that have anything to do with the feral brain, missing crew, and broken wraiths?

There was no way to tell from this room, or anywhere else in Pod Q.

"We need to reach Grid at Pod A," Alto said. They wondered how much good that would do if that lashing brain had destroyed every wraith besides Zelany, but at least they might find answers. "If we get there, I can fix central comms."

"A traveling act, now you're talking," Zelany said. He

34

snaked across the room and paused beside the door. "Let's get this show on the road."

Alto glanced to the drawer beneath their bed. They should probably get dressed, but their feet remained planted in hesitation. Between anxious inner snow, intrusive suggestions, and now the threat of some feral brain hacking their thoughts, Alto's mind sometimes didn't feel like their own.

And yet when baring their body, its uncovered skin and surgical scars, Alto knew at least this much was theirs. No one would change that.

Still, they would hopefully run into crewmates, and none of them would appreciate this perspective. Alto hurried into black pants, boots, and a loose tank, and then threw on a dark coat they'd received when first joining the starship's crew. A feisty-looking yellowjacket emblazoned the back, the starship's corporate-mandated mascot. Pod A would hold manual patch tools, but Alto slung their synth-leather toolbelt around their waist just the same, in case they ran across anything to fix along the way.

Or anything looking to fight. Only security officer Praise carried real weapons; Alto would have to make do with a screwdriver or hammer.

At one last scan over the room, Alto spotted their harmonica in its wall cubby, the brass marked by Esme's fingerprints. Alto snatched it up and slid it into a spare toolbelt notch. A little music might not go a long way inside a damaged starship, but even nameless and forlorn songs might settle the nerves. Besides, there was no telling when Alto might return to Pod Q.

If, added the bad side of their brain. *If there's a return.*

They glanced to Zelany, whose cartoon display face winked, and then stepped into the hall.

4

The Yellowjacket owed some aspects of its design to the trains of old Earth, humanity's birthplace wielding influence over human shape and thought even in distant star systems. Most necessary components for life support and space travel were part of the Bridge in Pod A, like a train's engine. Interlocking compartments formed the rest of the starship pods, similar to train cars, except connected by pipes, wires, wraith-ports, and interlocking doorways to make them appear seamless within, each fitted with at least a tiny airlock and space gear in case of decoupling. Merchant Guild decided the size of the starship based on each crossing's necessity and relabeled the pods as needed.

For this crossing, the Yellowjacket ran from Pod A to Pod T, forming a lengthy cylinder through space. Somewhere in the middle sat twin cargo holds, while another two sat at the rear, each carrying two hundred and fifty corpses. The pods' interlocking systems were uniform, but their insides came in all shapes. Some pods stretched into open rooms like Pod G's kitchen and dining area, while Pod O's zig-zag halls twisted around a mess of pipework, and narrow walkways overlooked the Yellowjacket's grim cargo in Pods K, L, S, and T.

Reaching Pod A from Pod Q meant traversing most of the ship, one long walk down these train cars through space.

Alto followed Pod Q's ring-shaped hallway until they reached the exit to Pod P, another quarters section. Its gray walls broke into four bedroom doors plus the airlock and two exits to neighboring pods. Every surface hummed with life support systems. The ceiling opened around small yellow lights, and the usual starship chill coated the air.

Alto slipped their small hammer from toolbelt to hand and gave the nearest wall a few noisy taps. Tinny echoes clanged through Pod P, but no doors slid into walls and no heads popped out shouting to keep the noise down. Alto touched the nearest door, found it locked, and then walked the dark floor, trying each room.

The hall was voiceless, silent. No one emerged. Nothing in sight except half a dozen shiny bits on the floor, maybe fragments from another broken wraith.

Alto didn't expect to find anyone but needed to perform the futile role of searcher to stall what came next. So long as they kept busy, nothing bad could happen, same as when they were a child who had hurried into a chore upon overhearing their parents caught in a storm of bad moods. Neither Mom nor Father would interrupt Alto's sweeping snow from the doorstep or cleaning scrap parts with pointless shouting or swatting, or else the work might pause. Alto was good at finding new chores.

Too busy for bad moods, too busy to think. Or overthink.

Alto hadn't reminisced on their childhood in some time. Maybe nostalgia was normal in crisis situations. Soldiers of warships like Archon Triumph and Archon Devourer might have thought more of their childhoods than of bloodshed when both ships slaughtered the L.K. Purity during the last cross-faction war. Alto had watched from an opportunistic Merchant Guild vessel's viewport. Guild analysts had stood nearby and studied how best to profit from both sides' individual weaknesses and mutual hatred. That was the guild way.

Parents. Battles. Both sets of memories shook down Alto's spine. Too much stalling would not help them now.

Zelany scraped along the hallway's curve on his tail and paused at the exit to Pod O.

"Can you scan for human life in the quarters rooms?" Alto asked.

A white sheen flashed across Zelany's interface. "I'm no casting director, but this audition's a ghost town."

No people, but no signs of struggle either, wraith parts aside. If an alarm had roused everyone aboard and Alto had slept through it, why hadn't Esme woken them up?

She must have gone back to her room beforehand. Even if she'd hated her time in Alto's bed, there was no way she'd let them sleep through an emergency.

Unless she hated Alto, too—no, the bad side of their brain couldn't have that satisfaction.

"Want me sneak ahead and gauge the crowd?" Zelany asked. His display showed his cartoon face peeking from between bulky scarlet curtains.

Alto eyed the wraith-port a few feet from the exit to Pod O. Slender channels ran through the length of the ship, with at least two exit ports per pod. They could lead Zelany all the way to Pod A.

"Check ahead," Alto said. "But come back if there's trouble."

"Caution is advised when everyone's a critic." Zelany dropped to his belly and slithered into the wraith-port. His flicking tail echoed the feral brain's tubes, steel instead of flesh.

Alto paced toward the opening to Pod Q, where another wraith-port opened in the dark wall. No fluid or residue. The brain hadn't emerged in this pod. It might have scurried farther up the ship, bleeding all the way.

What exactly had Alto done to it? Psionic nodes let the wraiths communicate between each other, better than any general wireless tech. Mind to mind to Grid, pieces of the ship's body. The feral brain had grabbed Alto's mind and shaken it like the glitter-filled snow globes Co-Captain Ying liked to collect. Once the node had fallen into flesh, Alto had grabbed the brain in return and shaken back. Thought against thought. Psionics might only be benign in wraiths' heads, but dangerous in the heads of others.

Not every Yellowjacket crewmate had augmentation wires in their skulls, and it seemed unlikely even then that they might plant wraith-nodes in their foreheads. What would happen if they met the feral brain?

"Jumping to conclusions," Alto muttered, lost again in their mind's inner snow.

The brain pest and the crew's absence could be unrelated problems. Maybe no one else had encountered the visitor. Alto had only gathered the Yellowjacket's circumstances in bits and pieces given by Zelany. Some ship called the Star-Hopper had landed on a planet. Grid had picked up their distress call and forced it through communications as per protocol of Merchant Guild, Luminous Kingdom, and most other interplanetary factions. The Yellowjacket must have answered.

Strange that Captain Sajid of the Star-Hopper hadn't mentioned any faction affiliation. A private vessel? Scrappers, smugglers, pirates? Protocol directed the Yellowjacket respond unless involved in emergency or war, faction be damned, but the lack of affiliation made Alto wonder.

A tinny rattling echoed along Pod P's hallway ring. Alto paced toward the Pod O exit as a black mask shot from the wraith-port, its green avatar flashing wide-eyed panic across its interface.

"Tough crowd, tough crowd!" Zelany cried. He hit

the floor and snaked past Alto.

Wet slapping struck the wraith-port's edge as it poured a grotesque flower of writhing tubes into the pod. Something pink and gray slid behind the limbs, onto them, its wrinkled surface gleaming in the dim light. Black ichor congealed between its folds, souvenirs of a psionic fight with Alto.

The feral brain.

5

A spinal tremor tugged Alto back two steps, and their heels knocked against Zelany's tail. No amount of Esme-driven therapy sessions would ready Alto for seeing a tentacled brain slip out of a hole in the wall. They could only swallow their revulsion and face it.

Purple light crept through the pod, a fresh coat of paint meant to dip Alto down another sinister vision.

How had they fought it off last time? The violent brain had pushed, and Alto had pushed back, almost a reflex, like the jerk of banging their elbow on their bed's corner. They let the brain try hacking their mind again, a heavy prying weight, and then they tensed against it.

Wrinkles flexed at the brain's front, and it recoiled into its tubes. Did it remember this sensation? The force of someone who could fight back?

"Get back in the wraith-port," Alto snapped. "Leave

us alone."

Zelany jittered against the backs of Alto's knees. "Look out, star, they got rotten tomatoes too."

They. And not the way Alto used the word. Their heart quickened, recalling Zelany's panicked scramble out of the wraith-port. He would have said *heckler* had he meant only one problem, but he hadn't.

He'd said *crowd*.

A lance of purple light sprang from the wraith-port as another brain emerged into the hall. Large as the first, its tubes seemed thicker, longer, as if Alto had only faced a juvenile brain and now its parent had reared its ugly head to protect is young.

Purple acid devoured the walls. They would soon collapse either to open space or some impossible nightmare.

Alto tensed against the psionic onslaught, but now thought against thought seemed a losing fight. The brains could hack minds as a unit, produce some larger illusion, maybe strong enough to break through any node-influenced defense. Nimble fingers squeezed Alto's hammer. These creatures looked soft, breakable in a real-world way.

Sharp claws raked glassy snow through Alto's thoughts, and the hammer slipped from their hand. They didn't hear it hit the hard floor. Only scraping in their head, only screams.

A third brain emerged from the wraith-port. Longer tubes? Greater bulk? Alto couldn't tell anymore, only felt the dark lump creep closer, weighing on their thoughts. The pod walls climbed—no, Alto went sinking to their knees. To the floor, same as the last time they'd faced a feral brain.

Pod P's dim ceiling melted into a wider circle of familiar white lights, now tinted a dull maroon. Techs, nurses, and doctors flitted through room and hall in a complex dance of life and death. Alto sat up from a lopsided bed, tubes jutting from one arm, hair shaved off their head and below the waist.

They knew this place. The surgery wing at Atlantica Prime, how many crossings ago? A beautiful day turned heavy as flesh-and-suture reality had come crashing in. Admins slipped by with papers and screens, piling on anxieties of long-term debt, the kind that would force Alto into communications work on mining asteroids, corpse ships, that stint at the nightmarish cerebrator lab the one and only time Alto had taken payment from the Luminous Kingdom. Genuine problems.

But hollow problems followed, dressed in clever skin suits as if they were the real thing. The bad side of Alto's brain had grabbed up paranoid thoughts of rusted hooks scratching through skull bone, a chest splayed open by needles and surgical drills, and a spine rent asunder by an enormous pair of scissors, its blades nicking every vertebrae from neck to tail bone. Symptoms of Alto's cold irrational anxiety, but real then before the anesthesia had taken over.

Real again now. Inner snow fed this purple hell, and

soon it would avalanche into another Perfect Alto Fuck-Up, this time costing their life.

"But it isn't—" Alto hissed. They made to grab for their head, but their limbs weighed a thousand pounds. "Can't be real."

Surgeons stormed the room in dark purple hoods and light purple aprons splashed with maroon streaks. Their violet-gloved fists clutched rusty hooks bent into cruel question marks, each asking if Alto really wanted their body pulled apart.

They couldn't open their mouth fast enough; these surgeons did not wait for answers. A hooked point dug into the left sleeve of Alto's black-and-yellow coat. A grunt and a tug, and the hook drew back a twisted knot of gooey tissue stretched through the coat's hole. Another surgeon plunged his hook into the back of Alto's skull and twisted the point deep. The patient was the prize, and these doctors would drag Alto into the surgery bay by their skin if need be.

Had this happened to the rest of the Yellowjacket's crew? They might not have died in their quarters or run to Pod A, at least not of their own free will. No need for the captain to sound the alarm and draw the crew into one place when these brains and their mind-hack could herd people wherever they liked. They only needed a bad memory, an irrational fear, anything. Human minds came stuffed with glass shards; a little shaking, and they would wound themselves.

What about inhuman minds?

46

Cruel hooks hauled Alto toward blood-painted hallways, but outside the illusion, the brains and their tubes crept closer across Deck P. Surgery had come and gone years ago, and it had never worn the face of this nightmare. There was a world outside this vicious mind-hack. Yellowjacket, a crossing, pod walls, wraiths.

The node stung against Alto's forehead. Time to be stronger. A deep breath, in and out. The brain was to blame, but it held sweeter memories too.

Yes, anxiety had haunted the early hours of surgery day, but when the time came, a procedure that had passed in hours for the surgeons swept by Alto in a singular black hole of a moment. They had drifted off and also awoken in an instant, no dark tunnel or dreams between, only riding a bend in time.

Some technician or nurse had warned Alto that they would be sore for a few days in head, chest, and between the legs. True, but Alto had emerged giddy.

The changes were right, what Alto had always needed, and now they had it. Easy to pass off the excisions up top to the occasional lover as a biological convenience, or the flesh and machine below the waist as a fancy toy, but in the truth of both cases, Alto's joy came first. They owned this body better than they owned their mind, and every change flowed from that oneness. Their chest had not suited them, but now it did. The shape between their legs had felt incomplete, but this fluid complexity brought bodily unity on an organ-deep level. Both upper scars and lower augmentation became an extension of self, as one with Alto as their fingers, their tongue.

The procedure's cranial wiring had saved Alto from the first invasive assault, and now these monsters wanted to tear out the sanctity of those memories. The surgery was beautiful in its cutting and scars and the cozy sense of wholeness. These hateful little shits had only ugliness inside. They had no right to Alto's head.

One deep breath, and then another, and Alto pried their mind open harsher than any skin-tugging hooks. Through the purple-clothed surgeons and the grisly never-was surgery wing—there, the Yellowjacket's pod in its dim lights, and wraith parts, and the brains looming nearer.

Time to see how they liked their nightmares thrown back at them.

Alto lunged, their mind carrying a world of purple horrors, a thought so violet. No pain or excitement spread through tender tangled wires. No inner snow. Alto only knew the purity of fighting back for what was theirs.

The vision thrust from their head and struck the three brains, each mind splitting open to let in a violet-tinted cathedral of gore.

Again with this image. It didn't belong to Alto, same as their surgery didn't belong to any feral brain. They must have found it in each creature's mind, a mutual memory between each brain. Either they had all experienced it together, or they'd felt it under some pre-Alto psionic attack when they had last met someone they

48

shouldn't have fucked with.

Alto didn't know, didn't care. They only wanted these things gone.

Another push, and the cathedral of gore stretched wider in the feral brains' minds. A dark silhouette darted across Alto's vision and in between those carnal walls. Was that Esme's beautiful figure? Alto had no idea; it was only an illusory shadow dashing down the cathedral as if planting a ghost in the brains' thoughts. Alto hoped to haunt each one.

Pressure eased from their mind, and their sight snapped back to the hall's gray-and-white gloom. No purple lingered here, or at least Alto didn't see it.

They only saw the brains buckle and retreat toward the wraith-port. Shadow-black fluid leaked down their frontal folds as they bumped against each other. They were disoriented, aching.

Alto snatched the hammer off the floor in a dry metal scrape and charged for the far wall.

One creature dove into the wraith-port; another began to follow. Too many. Too slow.

The hammer's head crashed into the last creature's lumpy side. Fluid spattered, and the chest-sized brain smacked wetly against the floor. Bits of blood sprayed beneath the hammer's second blow.

Not nearly enough. Alto dove onto their knees, raised the hammer two-handed, and slammed its head into the meat a third time. The feral brain's surface was slick, but the blow landed. Alto raised the hammer again and pounded another hard strike. Meat resisted, and then another blow, and the flesh flattened, and then caved in, and craters patterned the fallen brain as if beaten by an enraged meteor shower. Once-grasping tubes drooped into limp red snakes along the floor as a coppery stink filled in the air.

6

Alto slid back on sticky red hands, and they were glad to have dressed in a dark outfit. The blood wouldn't be so obvious. They weren't sure why that mattered when everyone else on the ship might be dead.

Something scraped the floor, and Alto whirled, hammer raised—only Zelany, creeping closer now that the danger was gone.

"Are you hurt?" Alto asked. But that wasn't the right word. "Damaged?"

"No bad review can get me down," Zelany said, his voice bouncy. "The show must go on." That would have to count for a positive answer.

Alto toed one boot against the brain—no twitching, no purple visions. Either it was dead or close enough. Red slime dribbled over the floor, one final means for the brain to reach for Alto and Zelany.

"I thought it might shoot out some big psychic blast when it died," Alto said. "Did you see any of that? The surgeons, the—" They stopped. Saying *cathedral of gore* out loud felt like too much.

"Sounds like a private screening, champ," Zelany said.

No, then. The first feral brain had assaulted Alto's mind before they'd had any chance of landing a psionic node in their head. They wondered what Esme had seen when she'd wandered off. Not illusory surgeons, but some nightmare unique to her thoughts.

Wraiths seemed immune. But why smash them then? Why not ignore them?

"Wraith-ports seem too risky right now," Alto said. "You'd better stick with me."

"Hands-on management for my star." A green hand appeared on Zelany's screen and stroked his cartoon face's chin. "Not a bad gig."

Alto slid the hammer onto their toolbelt, wiped both palms on their thighs, and led through the door to Pod O. Blue light coated the narrow pipe-filled halls in a serene hue as if to offset the clanking machines at work treating the starship's recycled water supply. The main corridor branched off in a dozen places, and each branch twisted around the machines. Most were too narrow even for Alto, designed so wraiths could perform maintenance under human supervision.

But not anymore. Another broken wraith lay tangled in the main corridor to the next pod, its tail cracked in several places, its wraith-plate dented into its sternum, and the wires severed between its spine and somehow intact black mask. This one had probably been helping Elvis check the recyclers before he disappeared with the rest of the Yellowjacket's crew. These brains had a hate-on for wraiths, as if their immunity to mind-hack were a personal rejection.

Not that the brains treated humans much better.

"Weird they can interface with our minds in the first place," Alto said, kneeling beside the broken wraith. Their fingers prodded the interface, a hopeless effort. "Aliens should be entirely incompatible, right? And we're aliens to them. It's odd."

"Understudies read the same script," Zelany said, peering over Alto's shoulder. "Same role, new performance, but that's show biz, baby."

Alto let this sink in. Same script, new performance, like hacking human thought. The feral brains might see it all as psionic junk anyway. Everything the first feral brain had forced into Alto's head had seemed general—shadows and falling, nothing intimate—while the trio of brains had dredged personal fears from Alto's memory. The hacked human provided the weapon. Minds full of glass.

Wraiths had no thoughts to hack outside their circuitry. Did that immunity come off as a threat, even though wraiths were harmless? Linking a wraith-node to Alto's mind may have turned them into something far worse than the feral brains had ever expected.

Good.

The broken wraith's black interface lit under Alto's fingertips. White-noise fuzz filled the screen, an automatic sign of error, and no start-up sound chimed from its speakers.

"Looks like this one's ready for Hollywood Forever," Zelany said.

Alto didn't know what that meant. The wraith was broken, but some part of it still wanted to function.

Another fingertip's stroke, and the white fuzz sharpened at the mask's center. Each forehead node lit in a one, two, three sequence until each glowed, and then the static cut away, leaving a face in the screen's center. Not a cartoon avatar or Alto's reflection.

Esme.

Her arms stretched to either side of the screen. Sweat drops shined from her face, and a red film coated her hair as if a slimy tube had tried to grab it. Her blouse was misbuttoned, and a mysterious stain coated one side.

She was the best thing Alto had seen since waking up.

"I can't go back," Esme said, her face pressing near the screen. "They're everywhere."

Alto pulled the wraith's mask close. "You don't need to go back. Tell me where you are, and I'll come to you."

Esme exhaled hard, fogging the screen. "Alto, if you're seeing this, I'm sorry. Everything happened so fast."

Alto's heart sank. Esme wasn't transmitting from one wraith to another. This was a recording. Still, she was alive, or at least she had been when she recorded this message.

"They're using the wraith-ports," Esme said. "I'm not sure if every wraith's been wrecked, but far as I can tell, Grid's gone down. The Yellowjacket answered that distress call, and we don't know what's happened since." She wiped one arm down her face. "Listen, someone set the ship into lockdown from Pods A through F. I don't know if the plan's to jettison Pods G through T or tow them floating behind us."

Alto gave a nervous giggle. Jettisoning the cargo would never fit Merchant Guild's protocol, brain aliens be damned. Any guild member must have lost their mind to think they'd get away with that.

A stern, familiar voice beckoned from off-screen. "We got to go!" That was security officer Praise.

"One second," Esme said, glancing over her shoulder. She leaned closer to the screen. "Look, only Captain Day can release the lockdown once it's underway, and no one's seen her. I mean, I haven't, neither has Praise. There's no choice but to ride this out. Alto, if you're seeing me now, don't let those things twist up your head. Find a distraction, plow on to Pod F, and don't let anything stop you."

Esme closed a hand over the screen, and the recording snapped to black.

Alto leaned the wraith's mask back. Transparent residue dotted its interface. Was this skin oil? How long ago had Esme crouched here, recording her message? A few minutes? An hour or more? The video hadn't shown a ship-time signature, and Esme hadn't given a lockdown timetable. Maybe she didn't know it.

Maybe Alto was already too late to reach Pod F.

That was no way to operate. Esme had said to hurry, so Alto would hurry. Nothing else to be done. They set down the wraith's head and stood again.

Zelany went rigid at Alto's side. His cartoon avatar flashed a flat expression, and a toneless feminine voice spoke through his interface: *One hour until lockdown.*

Perfect, yes, exactly what Alto needed to know. As if the Yellowjacket had heard their desperate thoughts, Zelany had picked up the signal and handed it over. Alto could have hugged him. Emergency alerts must have routed through Grid's subsystems, same as air, heat, and gravity, as a failsafe against comms troubles.

"An hour's plenty," Alto said, their new smile beaming eternal. "From here to Pod F, catch up with whoever's left of the crew. Praise. Esme, I hope."

Zelany coiled back. "You sure she's still got a part in this production?"

"I'm not." Alto glanced up Deck O's twisting pipe-laden corridors. "But the goal's the same—Pod A. So long as we hit Pod F before the lockdown."

"Sounds like Grid's not running this show anymore," Zelany said.

"No, but if we make Pod A and I fix the comms center, we can take the Star-Hopper's distress call and amplify it," Alto said. "I don't know if we're too late for their crew, but someone else could still help us." They started down Pod O's main hall, where a door slid open to Pod N. "Whatever's left of us."

Best to hope that meant everyone on the Yellowjacket. Esme, Praise, Jissika, Elvis, Dr. Calhoun, Captain Day, and Co-Captain Ying. And Alto and Zelany, too.

If they reached Pod F before the lockdown.

THE MESSENGER

7

The entrance door to Pod N slid shut as a hard thump rang in Alto's ear. They paused, eyed Zelany—he hadn't collided with the wall—and then glanced over their shoulder.

The thump came again. Muffled, almost distant, but too loud to be Alto's imagination. Could the water treatment be working overdrive to push fluid toward the front pods before lockdown? Unnecessary when Pod D also specialized in water treatment. Pod O only existed to provide treated water to the quarters pods without overtaxing the Yellowjacket's power cores.

A third thump—closer now. Zelany had scanned for human life in the quarters and come up empty, but Dr. Calhoun might have been checking the rear twin cargo holds in Pods S and T, or Elvis had needed supplies from Pod R, or some other optimistic crew-related fantasy.

Better to plow ahead, no matter who or what followed. Esme hadn't waited for Alto, good on her. Alto wouldn't wait either.

Especially if that wasn't a crewmate thumping up the pods.

Pod N's lounge opened in a tight box where floor and furniture grew from one molded chunk of immovable hard alloy. A dark table to one side doubled for a game screen, and a strip of three-inch tall, three-foot wide window cut one wall.

Scuff marks patterned the floor, and mangled wiring jutted from one wraith-port on the far side, but otherwise, the lounge looked pristine and unlived in. Nowhere on the Yellowjacket took on a personal touch outside crew quarters. Service wraiths excelled at clean-up. This quiet place should have flooded Alto with memories of crew gatherings for games, snacks, chatter, but the Yellowjacket had grown too long these past crossings and its meager population stretched too thin, a skeleton crew for the corpse loads. Only the ghosts of would-be memories haunted here, none of the real thing.

Small wonder Alto and Esme hadn't shared a real out-of-session conversation until now.

When nobody needed a comms specialist, Alto would sometimes sit beneath the window, let their eyes soak up the stars, and play whatever music came floating through their harmonica's reed plates.

There wasn't time for gentle music and pretend company right now, but Alto leaned toward the wall and looked out on twinkling blackness anyway.

The faintest maroon curve peeked from the window's corner, hinting at a world. The Yellowjacket must have chased the Star-Hopper's signal to its source and slipped into the planet's orbit.

Had anyone taken a shuttle to the surface? A rescue mission to extract the Star-Hopper's crew might have already been underway before these brain aliens had infiltrated the Yellowjacket. Maybe the rescue was done, and there were more people aboard now, which didn't explain the loud thumping, but Alto wanted it to.

A finished rescue might explain how the brains had boarded the Yellowjacket in the first place. Shuttles had no wraith-ports, but gaps spread between pipes and wires, and though the creatures were larger than human brains, they made squeezing into small spaces look easy, as if they were rodents. Their infestation could have spread from planet to Star-Hopper to Yellowjacket. The crew would have to make sure none followed onto whichever ship answered the amplified distress call once Alto and Zelany reached Pod A and comms.

Another thump sent Zelany slithering between lumps of furniture until he reached the door to Pod M. "We botch this rehearsal, the company's likely to saddle you with a new co-star," he said.

Alto followed through the lounge and exit doorway. Their fingers tapped the harmonica at their toolbelt, as if meaning to take another look out the slender window and play one forlorn note. Better they wait for now and then play for Esme when they found her.

Onward.

Pod M was smaller than Pod N, a narrow hall broken up to either side by vacant monitors overlooking desks of clipped papers and magnetized pencils. When the Yellowjacket reached its destination, Merchant Guild accountants and foremen would peruse this office and the cargo holds to ensure every corpse had reached the wraith processing facility.

If the Yellowjacket reached its destination. Alto wished to swat that two-letter word out of their head. No room in this skull for *if.*

Another thump jostled the pods, either from Pod O's edge or already pounding its way into Pod N. Did it cross the pods by doorways or scuttle through wraith-port channels? Maybe the thumper was headed for Pod F, eager to beat the lockdown same as Alto, if not for the same reasons.

Lockdown threat ahead, thumping threat behind. Best to hurry. Even if someone found the captain, she would be unlikely to lift the lockdown. A crew never knew when they needed to shut out mercenaries, or pirates, or Luminous Kingdom zealots.

Or aliens, apparently. A starship vermin like none encountered before.

Alto strode through the exit to Pod L, Zelany on their heels, and slowed as the door slid shut behind them. A slender steel-and-iron walkway clanged underfoot, overlooking one of the Yellowjacket's cargo holds. The tail of a broken wraith tangled with the railing to one side, its mask shattered against the floor, its skull facing down as if mourning the cargo. Pod L offered nowhere for the feral brains to hide; they must have beaten the wraith and moved on.

The rounded white ceiling hung low, close enough for a taller person than Alto to touch, while generous floorspace sagged beneath the walkway. From outside the ship, Alto had thought the cargo holds looked like bulging egg sacks at the center and rear of a monstrous insect.

But these were not eggs, full of new life. Shelves upon shelves of corpses filled the Yellowjacket's four cargo pods.

Whenever asked by Co-Captain Ying, Merchant Guild reps, or even Praise, Alto had said they were used to the sight. The lie made Alto hirable and the crossing easier to bear.

But with Esme, lying would have wasted precious session time. Better to admit the corpses chilled Alto's blood. Better to admit they crossed Pods L, K, S, and T without looking down if they could help it. Comms had only broken here last time the door between cargo holds malfunctioned.

It looked to be malfunctioning now, a half-lidded sideways eye offering glimpses to Pod K, as if the door were a corpse's eyelid someone had forgotten to shut before sealing the dead in protective hard casing.

Someone looked to have forgotten the hard casing entirely. On an ordinary crossing, corpses would lay side by side in orderly rows of reusable containers to await processing. The Merchant Guild techs would open the cargo airlock at the bottom of each hold, and then one by one the corpses would slide through a digestive system of circuits and saws and psionic nodes until they emerged as usable wraiths.

This was no ordinary situation. Distress calls were typical, as was the protocol for responding to them. Brain aliens were an unprecedented circumstance, but not impossible; millions of undiscovered species had to dot the cosmos.

What lay below did not make sense. Could not make sense.

Alto grasped the walkway railing, and their knuckle bones shone through skin like featureless white faces smothered beneath sienna cloth.

Pod L's cargo hold teemed with trembling flesh. The lids hung open from each corpse's hard casing, exposing their once-pressurized carcasses to the air. The feral brains might have triggered some switch to open them, but that did not explain the tremor running through each corpse. Twisted dead faces twitched, limbs batted against plastic, and their mess of flesh jittered over the floor.

Were they alive? That couldn't be; they had been dead when brought aboard, gathered from different settlements across two worlds. None of them stood up, let alone shouted to Alto that there'd been a mistake. Had unseen feral brains lashed into Alto's head with another mind-hack? Alto looked for signs of purple and found only patches on the corpses' decaying flesh.

Zelany peered through the railing and scanned the cargo. "Better chat with the props department," he said. "They're making sets for the wrong production. We can't use these."

He was right. Whatever power had stirred these corpses, there would be no making wraiths of them now. Their flesh lay exposed.

"Stop moving anyway," Alto whispered to the dead.

A thump answered from beyond Pod M's doorway. From Pod N? Unlikely Alto would have heard it then. The thumper had reached Pod M and would soon hit Pod L.

Critical rot had seeped through the M.G. Yellowjacket while Alto slept. Time to cross the walkway, the next cargo hold, hurry to Pod F. Nothing else mattered. Alto wrenched their gaze from the restless corpse heap and started for the fluttery broken door to Pod K.

Dark shapes lingered beyond the door's twitching sideways eyelid. Chest-wide lumps, their surfaces wrinkled, hid to either side with one obscured by door, the other by wall.

Waiting.

Alto slid back a step, banging their heel into Zelany's tail. "Keep behind me."

"I can take a stage direction," Zelany said. "These paparazzi are all yours, star."

Any minute now, Pod L would welcome scuttling tubes and purple illusion. Would the feral brains' next mind-hack toss Alto back into a nightmarish surgery wing? Would they try another pit? Some new trick? Alto tensed, their mind ready to fight.

The cargo hold chilled, and a hollow tapping filled the air. Not the thumper in Pod M, but the corpses, their prone bodies jerking and colliding with their hard cases and each other.

Alto watched the doorway to Pod K. Neither brain moved. Doubtful they were dead. Had they figured out that Alto was stronger? Three of the damn things couldn't win in Pod P, and Alto had killed one. These might be the last.

A chair pounded at a desk back in Pod M. The thumper, almost here. It would come pounding through the door and send the steel walkway floor clanging under its railing.

Violent snowfall haunted the bad side of Alto's brain—if the aliens meant to ambush, why wait where Alto could see? One could've hidden in some nearby wraith-port and hacked Alto's mind before they knew it. Instead, both brains sat with eternal patience and visibility in Pod K as if to say, *Come and get us*.

As if their presence wouldn't make Alto's nerves scream, *Trap*.

A genuine trick, or another kind of illusion, the brains pretending to set a trap solely to stall Alto? Enough indecision, and both Alto and Zelany would miss the lockdown.

But how the hell could these creatures understand the

Yellowjacket's situation? More likely they meant for Alto to freeze here and let the thumper catch up on the walkway. It would bash Zelany next, same as the broken wraith tangled up in the railing, and then it would try for Alto.

"Enough," Alto snapped.

The bad side of their brain would swirl them lost in a whiteout blizzard, paralyzed with indecision. The lockdown allowed no time for mind games, no time to stall on two Pod K-dwelling brains while another snuck up from behind, already thumping through the door, onto the walkway.

Alto's teeth sawed molar against molar. No more tricks. They would handle the thumper, and then the feral brains ahead, and anything and everything that stalled the way to Pod F, and then to Pod A.

"Stay close," Alto said, guiding Zelany to their side as they around toward Pod M. "Be ready for whatever comes."

Zelany replied, but whatever he said came muffled. Not under a loud thump—that noise had ended—but a stray note caught in Alto's ear as if someone had begun to play a stranger's harmonica beside their head.

The Pod M door slid shut behind a familiar figure, and gentle steps blocked out the sound of smacking corpses below.

Esme had stepped onto the walkway.

8

Relief sent Alto rushing down the walkway, arms open. Were they on hugging terms with Esme? They'd hugged after a couple counseling sessions, they'd had sex, but—this was ridiculous, like every anxious thought in Alto's head. They jogged toward Esme and wrapped one arm around her waist, the other around her shoulder.

Esme hummed. "You're okay," she said, astonished.

Alto almost said, *And you weren't some monster chasing me*, and then laughed in Esme's ear.

Not a monster, and Esme was alive, each a welcome revelation. She looked as she had in the wraith-mask's video, her blouse's buttons crisscrossed, her messy hair stained and sweaty and fantastic. She trembled in Alto's arms. The chaos aboard the Yellowjacket had eroded her confidence. Both she and Alto walked a thin glass bridge over the vacuum of space while violent brains armed with the drills and hooks of Alto's illusion chipped beneath their feet, bit by bit.

Alto looked into Esme's eyes. "Are you hurt?"

"Lonely," Esme said. "Afraid. Does that count?" She nuzzled her face into the black-and-yellow coat sleeve, and a chill shook her limbs.

Alto broke the hug to slip off their coat. "Take it. You left yours."

They'd left it, too, should have brought it in case they found Esme. Why hadn't Alto thought of that when leaving their room? Had they assumed Esme was dead? Now she was here, alive and cold, while her coat lay useless on the floor back in Pod Q. Her boots too. Bare feet pressed at the walkway, purple nails gleaming in the light.

Esme hung the coat over one arm and nodded down. "Boots off, too."

"They might be small for you," Alto said, but they did as they were told and slipped off the boots. Steel ran cold against bare soles.

Esme gave a slow nod. "All of it."

Alto's arms twitched, unsure where to go, what to do.

"All of it, I said." Esme dropped the coat, kicked past the boots, and pawed at Alto's clothes. The dark tank top climbed Alto's middle, snagged on their chin, their nose, and then lifted overhead and fell out of sight. Esme tore off Alto's toolbelt, and it clanged against the walkway.

Inner snow began giving way to clear weather in

Alto's head. They could let Esme finish undressing them, and their freed skin might form a presence bigger than their body, as if joining the air itself.

But the moment grew stark, easy to understand.

"You know how people in bad situations want comfort?" Alto asked. They pressed at Esme, wanting to slow her without hurting her, but she was determined. "There's a term for it, that immediate affection after trauma. I can't remember."

Heavy breath tore through Esme's lips. "Me neither."

"Whatever it is, I think you're that way now," Alto said, pressing Esme's hand away from the waist of their pants.

Esme scoffed. "How else would I be?"

She tore at her blouse like a hungry animal. A stray button broke free and clacked against the walkway, where it rolled beneath the railing and plummeted toward the writhing dead. Alto thought of it striking a corpse's eye, or descending a decayed throat, and buckled under gut-deep revulsion.

"Don't you remember?" Esme asked. Her blouse flew loose from her round beauty, and white pants slid down her white-pink thighs. "I'm not like other therapists. I'm a fun therapist."

She laid her hands on Alto's hips, nails jabbing skin, and then swung them both toward the walkway railing. Hard metal struck the small of Alto's back as a kiss slammed their lips. Esme tasted sweet, a sugar cube for the tongue.

Alto wrenched back, freeing the corner of their mouth. "You're upset."

"What, you're the expert now?" Esme giggled against Alto's face. Her eyes were wild, their violet irises brighter than any star. "I told you to stop letting that fickle brain of yours get you down."

Alto pressed at Esme's arm, desperate not to hurt her, and then gave a full-hipped thrust. Esme stumbled back and Alto followed. Her mouth gaped somewhere between audacity and surprise. Did she not understand? Survival sex had to wait.

Zelany watched from the walkway's middle, his cartoon display face furrowing his brow in concentration. His personality settings probably read this moment as a scene take for some made-up video. He had no better sense of urgency than Esme.

Alto raised pleading hands. "We need to hit Pod F right now. It really isn't the time for—this."

"When was it ever?" Esme asked. She kicked stray boots out of her way and shoved Alto against the railing again. "What do you think we are, two star-crossed lovers at the end of a long stretch of yearning? That you're entitled to tenderness? What did you think we did, in your room?"

The bad side of Alto's brain must have found a new snowstorm in Esme's cold tone. Icy patterns froze into the worst possible conclusions.

Alto swallowed. "We had a nice time."

"But why the nice time?" Esme asked, looming

closer. "These aren't the complicated feelings you want them to be. Most people are simpler than that, and you and I are no exception. We're stuck on a starship on a low-pop crossing. You're nice, and nice-looking, and you made bedroom eyes at me over our sessions, don't hide it. So, why not? I don't know if I'll ever see you again, and I don't know what else I'm supposed to do. I fucked you out of boredom."

A sick heaviness sank through Alto's insides. They reached down for their coat. Better to be away from here, away from her.

Esme smacked Alto's arm. "I'm your therapist; I work here. What did you think, we were in love?"

"Of course not," Alto said. "But that maybe you liked me. That we sparked."

"All those things can be true at once," Esme said. "And you know it, you think it, but the problem is, you don't like hearing it. So let's quit talking."

She lunged for another kiss, more desperate this time. A terror thrived inside her, and something else. Back in Alto's room, Esme had a sweat-and-sweet human taste. She seemed too sweet now, her lips laced with candy, more like memory than a genuine touch. Her flavor was the past, her words fearing the future, echoes to Alto's anxiety now given the voice and face of its enemy—a therapist.

As if that anxiety walked in Esme's place.

Zelany went on staring from beside the broken wraith. He might have slipped into a standby mode for when two

74

users spoke to each other, sure. But if not, he might be staring with uncertainty as to why Alto seemed to share a conversation with thin air, Esme's presence standing outside his registry.

Had her eyes always been this insistent violet? Had her fingernails and toenails always shown this intense shade of purple?

"Don't be a bore, Alto," said Esme's face, her voice. "Kiss me back, touch me. We're going to die, so why not enjoy the end and fuck again? Even the corpses know we're done for. Why do you think they're so eager to touch each other? Don't let them spoil the mood."

Alto pressed their back so hard against the railing that their lower spine ached. Mention the cargo, spoil the mood—the bad side of Alto's brain had kept that thought bottled up in their room with Esme. How could she know it now? The words seemed plucked from Alto's mind, same as the illusory surgeons in Pod P.

Not a violent mind-hack, but worse, an intimate one.

"Okay, you don't like me being pushy anymore," Esme said, retreating. Her words staggered out. "There's a little vengeance in you, huh? But you still like me. I can change, same as that thing between your legs. What, then? Tell me, and I'll do that instead. Anything you want. I need it, we both do."

The brains had tried neutral fears at first, but Alto beat them back, and then personal fears, and Alto had killed one of them. Now these monsters meant to twist personal joy into the kind of barbed wire found on mining colonies to keep scavengers out and workers in.

This Esme illusion might look soft, but she was a snare of steel teeth meant to catch and keep. Any angle was worth trying if the feral brains could use it to break into Alto's mind. Augmentation had helped Alto surface from the first mind-hack, and the node had given them a way to fight back, but anxiety was a subtle traitor, opening a fortress's side door to welcome intrusive thoughts and terrible premonitions. Didn't matter whether they were true or not. Again, to be human was to have a mind of glass shards. Give it a shake, and let the pain and blood run free.

Old terrors could hurt, but so could the betrayal of joy.

"We need a little fun before we die," Esme whispered. "Don't let the wrong thoughts get you down. Remember, the brain is to blame, nothing more. Your brain."

No, not Alto's brain. Other brains, past the far end of the walkway, partly hidden behind the broken door to Pod K. They had stayed out of Pod L, but they should have stayed out of Alto's head.

Fury ripped through Alto's thoughts. Their head tensed, the node likely glowing with new psionic rage. They tensed forward and thrust a new thought so violet— no, a thought so violent.

Through air, through Esme-like mirage, into its source. Violet walls would open, another dark chasm in an alien mind, the cathedral of gore spreading, spreading, spreading until it split some feral brain's thoughts in two. Break its mind with bad memories, and maybe the others would finally learn to leave Alto the hell alone.

No cathedral of gore appeared within the Esme mirage. The chasm instead stretched within her skin, a roof of bone rising and rounding until it formed the inside of a surgical theater. This small world filled with people in thin masks and operating gowns and gloved hands, all cloaked in purple.

The nightmarish hooks were gone. Instead, these surgeons wielded scalpels and clamps. Plastic-and-titanium bones dotted a nearby cloth-covered tray. Gloved hands dipped through skin and muscle, around real bones inside the lower back and hip of a teenage girl.

Tendrils of consciousness stirred through her mind. She was awake. Nothing like Alto's procedure when they had slid within a single moment. This girl lay half-anesthetized, aware and yet immobile, frozen in a night terror of blades and cutting and bone and fusing.

The surgeons had no idea. They chattered between each other as if performing an autopsy in the pre-wraith days of early star travel. Oblivious hands sank into the girl's body. They spread muscles and sinew. Jerked at cracked bones. Slid replacements inside. Soldered. Rewired. Pounded. Sawed.

She couldn't scream, or writhe, or run away. She felt every inner tug and fold and burn, trapped in a body of parts, as if it didn't belong to her. This was not Alto's dream of pre-surgery anxiety, but the nightmare of mid-surgery actuality. Memories Alto couldn't have known.

Dredged up from a real person.

9

Alto's mind drew back, easy as a slick knife. A mirage would have faded, but Esme grasped her head and sank wailing to the floor. The sound of her panic drowned out the ship's ambient hum and the endless smacking of corpses below—a scream, a breath, another scream.

"Esme?" Alto crept close and sank to their knees.

Another scream answered them, blowing hot breath in their face.

A light thump drew their eyes to the walkway's beginning. Either it had looked empty before as part of some illusion, or Alto had only paid attention to Esme, too distracted to notice what had followed her into Pod L.

The creature was distinct from any lone brain on tubes. Pink-gray wrinkles coated a faceless brain-like head as large as Alto's, stemming from a long neck and a narrow body. Its plump belly thumped against the floor, propelled in clumsy bursts by four stubby legs. It was an awkward three-foot beast of an alien brain. Its sightless head turned this way and that as if lost.

Zelany's metal tail clinked along the walkway as he slipped to one side. He said nothing, only doing as he'd been told, readying himself to hide behind Alto or else end up like his ravaged fellow wraiths.

Esme screamed again, and Alto wrapped their arms around her. Blouse buttons scraped at naked chest scars, but Alto didn't care. They'd messed up. The purple had only been Esme's eyes, her nails.

She was real.

"I'm sorry," Alto whispered. They almost thought they hadn't spoken, their words muffled under the jittering corpses and thumping brain-beast. "I didn't know it was really you. Esme, snap out of it, please?"

The next scream withered into a wail and then a long breath out Esme's lips. Alto cupped their hands around her face and peered into her eyes. She stared unblinking ahead, seeing no one. Her breathing shallowed.

Alto leaned closer and tensed their thoughts. They had only reached into the feral brains since the node's binding with living flesh, never another person, and only to lash out. This time, Alto slipped a purple hand into Esme's thoughts, a mind-hack meant to heal, but the sensation seemed to drift in some space-like emptiness. Nothing behind Esme's eyes, only a place as dark and broken as a wraith's cracked mask.

Why throw herself on Alto? Why taunt them? She might have come here panicked half out of her head, and Alto's psionics had shoved her the rest of the way. Or had the flopping brain-beast hacked Esme's mind, different physical shape from the others but the same mental assault? Every theory sounded like a guilty excuse.

Alto turned snarling from Esme. "What did you do to her?"

The brain-beast swayed with drunken confusion and then thumped another bellyflop closer, shaking the walkway's railing. It must have chased Esme here, clawing into her thoughts. Somehow it had turned her around after she'd left her video in Deck O's broken wraith, and then it had twisted hers and Alto's moment of joy against them.

"Has anyone ever done that to you?" Alto asked. "Got in your head and toyed around?" They leaned over their lap and tensed their thoughts at the brain-beast. "Want to know how it feels? How bad it hurts? I can show you."

The brain-beast's neck curved, paying no attention. A mind-hack would change that. Esme was right; Alto had a little vengeance in them, and they were willing to share.

The wraith-node glowed as Alto shot purple rage into the beast's mind. Its belly thumped again, sending a shockwave up the walkway, but Alto kept clawing. Somewhere inside lay that violet-tinged cathedral of gore.

Purple layers congealed within the brain-beast, first into echoes of mental surgeons, and then into segmented larvae spun in dizzying worm-like circles. Their torsos slapped together to the rhythm of the cargo's writhing corpses, and cruel illusory hooks clanged against the walkway railing.

Alto pushed through, the wraith-node screaming in their head. They had never thrust this hard against the feral brains, but this beast deserved to suffer for Esme. Through brain, surgeon-worms, into the depths, Alto's mind-hack sharpened to a mind-sword and carved open a gory mental chasm, seeking the brains' shared trauma of a meaty amphitheater within a broken starship. Something mewled as a wound opened in the brain-beast's mind.

No cathedral of gore stood in the violet haze. No surgical theater, either. No surgeons. A dark lake lapped behind the brain-beast's through, thick with maroon slop, wreathed in purple banks.

And there was a swimmer.

A hand climbed from the lake's muck, reached for the sword of Alto's mind, and curled its fingers beneath the blade. Alto tugged back like they'd slid from Esme, but the hand grasped firm. Either it couldn't be cut or it felt no pain.

That sense of a trap, a mistake slid again through Alto's head. Their nerves had shouted a warning about the ambush tucked in the next pod, but they should have been wary of these thoughts, this particular barbed-wire mind.

A muck-coated head surfaced from the lake. Two bright eyes glared from its dribbling face, a harsher violet than had ever stared from Esme. Another arm thrust from the maroon waters and grasped farther up Alto's mind-sword, closer to the hilt, to Alto, as a toneless voice breathed from the figure in the lake.

"You have opened yourself to the dark," it said, its pitch almost gentle. "And the dark gives itself to you. It gives you the Messenger."

Alto tugged again; no give. They visualized the mind-sword flying loose from the Messenger's grasp, maybe cutting those palms along the way, freeing Alto, but they couldn't make the vision a reality.

One hand released the blade only to grasp the hilt, where it touched some part of Alto. A finger crossed their thoughts, gently stroking. Another tug, but the mind-sword held firm, as if it were a real weapon stuck in the bones and innards of a real body.

"Look to me," the Messenger said, face creeping closer, dripping with dark sticky blood. "To face the Messenger is to embrace the Message."

Alto wanted to let go of the sword, but that would mean letting go of their mind. What would that do to them?

They tried thinking of the world outside this thought prison, the way they'd pierced the last mind-hack a few pods ago. Simple reminders—there was no lake, there was no sword. Alto actually stood on a janky walkway in Pod L, one of the M.G. Yellowjacket's middle cargo holds. Esme lay nearby, Zelany not far from her, and a wounded alien beast draped the floor ahead. No such thing as the Messenger. Only psionic fuzz, another mind-hack. Nothing more.

"You cannot deny me," the Messenger said, close enough to kiss. A finger-like sensation traced Alto's narrow face, their quivering jawline, the Messenger pretending to reach beyond the psionic, into the physical realm. "Even forgetting could not free you of me, and I will not let you forget. As mankind forever fears the dark, you will—"

Alto plowed deeper into the brain-beast's mind. If they couldn't draw back, they would thrust deeper, through, a little more, out the other side.

Their sight broke from the purple-tinged lake and onto Pod L of the Yellowjacket. Familiar white walls climbed to a low ceiling and sank to the trembling corpse pit below. Something smelled rank, likely the dead. A pink-gray beast lay writhing at the walkway's beginning. Esme gasped in shallow breaths a few feet behind Alto.

Zelany held tense to the railing, his speaker blaring a familiar warning: *Thirty minutes until lockdown.*

Alto stood above the beast, exactly as before. Not shaped like a sword, but as a human being. They breathed deep, coughed at the air's corpse-tainted scent, and shuffled back a step along the walkway's cold steel.

"—forever fear the vast unknown within," the Messenger said.

Alto jerked to one side and banged their hip against the railing. Someone else had entered Pod L.

A lithe figure crouched on the far railing. Dark violet

gore crawled down its skin, fat droplets falling toward the walkway but never striking it. Limbs as narrow as Alto's bent around its trunk, and its fingers and toes clung to the railing as they'd clung to Alto's mind.

Were still clinging. Alto hadn't escaped the mind-hack, or trap, or whatever the Messenger had to be. Its illusion persisted, a malevolent sketch on the real world. Alto's mind-sword had come back with gristle stuck to its blade, and now it stained their relaxed mind. No psionics needed. The Messenger was here, an illusion without end.

"You don't belong in my head," Alto said.

"I belong in you, and out of you, and everywhere," the Messenger said, almost proud. "I am the truth behind the universe, from which inspiration mankind sowed the seeds of torment in the fertile perceptions of their terrible minds, now nurtured and grown into nightmare thoughts within the mindscape of emptiness, endlessness, and death."

"We're not dying here!" Alto snapped. Purple tension ripped through their head and sailed toward the Messenger.

It stared unblinking. A stream of clot-filled blood dribbled past its narrow nose. It did not seem to breathe.

Alto tensed their head in another thrust, forming the mind-sword again, setting the wraith-node in their forehead glowing, digging and digging for a cathedral of gore.

But there was no presence on the railing. Nothing to crack open and find the glassy shards of memory. There was no mind to hack. The Messenger didn't crouch in the Yellowjacket; it clung to the insides of Alto's head and wouldn't let go.

"The vastness within cannot cast me out," the Messenger said. "Do you understand? You will not be alone anymore. Not even in your head."

Alto tried to retreat, but their back already pressed against the railing. "Zelany, scan psionics," they said.

Zelany's mask lit white, and then his cartoon Martian face blinked. "It's all you, champ. You're the star of this show, but you're belting your lines so loud, they can hear you in the next theater."

What did that mean? Maybe whatever muscle flexed inside Alto when unleashing their mind-hack could not now unflex. Their mindscape lay open for the taking.

The Messenger cocked its damp head. "I am no mind-hack."

"Stop knowing me!" Alto snapped. They grabbed their toolbelt off the walkway floor and slung it at the far railing. "Stop answering my mind!"

The Messenger watched the toolbelt clang against the railing, spit hammer, wrenches, and harmonica onto the walkway, and then drop into the writhing corpse pit. A disinterested expression turned to Alto. The Messenger let its gore drip down the frozen moment, and then it danced off the railing, closer, closer, until it disappeared into some vast darkness at the back of Alto's mind. Nothing to see, only to feel, as if Alto's anxiety had formed a new lake and the Messenger walked its shore.

"Stop," Alto grunted, grasping their head. "You're nothing. Brain static."

"I am no psionic intrusion," the Messenger said, their gentle voice ringing louder. "I am the dark, always with you, always with all. I bear the Message."

Alto shook their head hard, hoping to dislodge the darkness. It lingered, had always been there, as if the bad side of their brain cast a shadow. Except it couldn't; there was no *there* in Alto's head, so how could it host this psychic parasite?

Hands slid down the inside of Alto's skull. "I am no parasite. I am the Messenger."

"Okay," Alto whispered. "Okay, then give me the Message and get out of my brain."

"The Message is not given," the Messenger said, mirthful now. "It is absorbed and known, and through my presence, you will know it. You will know the dark."

The shadow swelled in Alto's mind, and their head went heavy as if they'd filled their skull with a broken starship. They sank beside Esme and banged their forehead against the walkway. One eye glanced from its corner toward Zelany for help, but wraiths were harmless, and besides, the Messenger had no form to fight. As far as Zelany could probably tell, Alto had lost their mind. Three wraith-nodes glowed with concern above his mask's useless cartoon avatar.

Wraith-nodes. Like the one Alto had thrust into their head by accident and used to push away the first feral brain. Another might strengthen that same psionic force.

Maybe enough to fight off the Messenger.

Alto pressed up from the floor and crawled in a brain-beast bellyflop. Along the railing, inch by inch, over Esme's sprawled legs. One desperate finger pointed to the broken wraith.

"Zelany," Alto said through gritted teeth. "The wraith-nodes."

A purple curtain blanketed the pod walls, and white dots glinted distantly in the blackness. Raw space seemed to twinkle in Alto's eyes.

"There is no end to me," the Messenger said, still gentle and yet impatient now. "I am the dark, and the dark opened your mind. You cannot escape the Message."

The unseen walkway again banged into Alto's forehead. Heaviness pressed skin and skull against metal flooring, and Alto worried the force might crush their wraith-node. Doubtful they would've lasted this long without it. Sweat dribbled into their eyes, staining the vast stretches of purpled space.

"It's not real," Alto whispered. "If I was out in the dark, I couldn't hear myself."

"But you're in here," the Messenger said. "With me."

A new electronic *ping* rang as an icicle drove through Alto's forehead, sharper and realer than any mind-sword.

The purple curtain thinned to a veil, and through it, Zelany reached a circuit-coated arm above Alto's eyes. Black wire dangled to the left, a wraith-mask's rubbery grapevine. One of its nodes had detected Alto's flesh and now burrowed inside to connect with its fellow node's wires, with the in-brain augmentation line.

With Alto's thoughts.

"You will not end me," the Messenger said, but its voice sank into its fading violet lake. "Your pain is without purpose."

The weight slid from Alto's skull and down their spine. They scrabbled off the walkway, one hand reaching for the wire hanging in Zelany's arm. Nothing else dangled from its ends.

"The other wraith-nodes," Alto said. "Where?"

"Broken," Zelany said. His interface closed cartoon eyes and shook his green head. "These budget cuts have been murder, I tell you."

Violet landscapes spread at the back of Alto's head. The Messenger wouldn't cower as easily as a feral brain; it would cling. Alto had to stop it. They sprang past Zelany in a loping half-crouch and bent against the broken wraith.

"The Message persists," the Messenger said.

Alto looked from inert black mask, down the wraith-plate, to the lengthy tail of metal vertebrae. Merchant Guild built wraiths from human remains and augmented them with cybernetic enhancements. They were more tech than organic, but their hardware set into the original frame. Unlike these aliens' brute force mind-hacks, every wraith part interfaced smoothly with human physiology, machine to corpse.

There was no need to differentiate between living flesh and the dead. A human was a human. A body was a body.

No anesthesia for this, and no time for stalling. Alto yanked a strip of circuity from the broken wraith's arm and drove it into their left bicep.

Bits of Merchant Guild tech sizzled and ticked, and then icy worms burrowed into Alto's flesh. Less painful than the nodes' installation, but Alto screamed anyway. Sometimes screaming felt better than nothing.

Skin folded around the new hardware like limp putty, as if Alto's flesh were already dead. Their body twitched and quaked, hating this, hating the universe as the circuitry augmented itself to muscle. They tried to ignore how these same wires and steel alloy had rooted in a dried corpse moments ago.

"You will not silence me forever," the Messenger said, quieter now. "You will know the Message."

Alto didn't answer, only tore loose another strip and drove it into their left forearm. And another, and another. Icy knives scattered down Alto's muscles, but each wiring nightmare seemed to drown out the rest, as if the human body could only process so much pain at once.

A soft voice sighed through violet darkness. "You will embrace the Message."

Alto braced their untouched arm against the broken wraith's torso and pried loose the wraith-plate. Circuits spat and dry flesh crackled as the grasping metal sprang off. Alto grasped it in both their unblemished hand and their circuit-strewn one, still jittering with the ongoing procedures, and then slammed the wraith-plate against their chest and abdomen.

Metal limbs clamped under armpits, around waist, over bellybutton and hip. The base touched above Alto's waistline, nearly linking with the old augmentation, the only one they had actually wanted. No point dwelling on regret right now; this was surgical survival. Wires drove through skin and sternum, under ribs, over organs. Its circuits met the arm, and the scrotal augmentation, and whatever connections climbed Alto's spine and let this mess work with their brain and the nodes set into their head. If any wire malfunctioned, there would be nothing Alto could do to fix it.

The last traces of the purple veil melted from sight. The shadow cast by the bad side of Alto's brain shrank beneath renewed clear weather. Whatever knelt and swam there faded, no violet intrusion to nourish its presence.

Only a whisper slid at the edge of thought. "The dark does not die in the light; it only waits," the Messenger said. "And I will wait. You will not be alone for long."

FLESH-HACK

10

Alto had never more appreciated peace in the Yellowjacket's ambient hum. The corpse cargo's writhing rhythm and Esme's gentle in-out gasps seemed almost silent after the Messenger's needle-in-mind incessance. Alto took a deep breath, let themselves have a moment.

The wraith-plate squeezed their ribcage. Its design didn't suit chests that expanded and contracted, but that was fine; Alto's body hadn't been ready for a metal hand to grasp their torso. Flesh and plate could get used to each other.

Alto climbed the railing overlooking the broken wraith, robbed of its functionality long before anyone came scavenging for parts. It wouldn't miss these.

Zelany slithered up the walkway. "A character actor," he said, his interface avatar scanning Alto up and down.

"Always a handful."

"I'll get everything removed when we make it out alive," Alto said. "Bacterial treatment, skin grafts, the works. In this deep, what's another thirty or forty thousand creds of medical debt?"

They tried to figure the math and cackled at impossible calculations. No idea how many more corpse crossings would drain the debt, or whether Merchant Guild might scrap and replace the whole wraith program after they learned of the Yellowjacket's fate. Most of the undead cyborgs had been less than useful against the feral brains, and Merchant Guild could make a killing if they threw a replacement on the market.

Riches for Merchant Guild, debt for Alto. Nothing new there.

Alto finished their cackle as another sensation itched deep inside. Not the wraith-plate on bare skin, but deep in their mind. New wirings needed time to get neighborly.

And something else hid beneath them. Despite the extreme new augmentations, the Messenger clawed at the underside of Alto's thoughts. Peace would not last forever. Alto's mind had never been less their own than right now. They looked over their half-naked body, raw with borrowed augmentations, one minor possession of flesh and bone.

At least this much was still theirs, not the Messenger's.

Alto stepped past Zelany and crouched beside Esme. Still breathing, still a pulse. She stared ahead into unwavering nothingness.

"You had Praise with you in your recording," Alto said. They reached for Esme's blouse and began to button it from bottom to top, skipping the spot where a button had flown off under Esme's relentless hands. "What happened to them?"

Only breath slid through Esme's lips. No words.

"The brains?" Alto asked, finishing with Esme's top button. "Is that why you panicked?"

Esme's pupils offered round portholes to stilled black space. Nothing to see or know, she floated apart from the universe. And that was Alto's fault. They had broken her.

"We can't stay," Alto said.

Their tank top must have slipped off the walkway; they didn't see it. They finished dressing Esme and then snapped up their coat and pulled it on. Ill-fitting around the wraith-plate, but they had no choice about that.

The peace broke apart in a pod-wide squelching, and a bad feeling sank down Alto's throat to their gut and through the floor, maybe into space itself. They shut their eyes.

You will know the dark, the Messenger had said.

"I won't," Alto whispered. They forced their head over the railing with open eyes, if only to defy the Messenger.

Shelves of cargo-dwelling dead flesh had spread across the floor and splashed against the walls in a corpse-strewn sea. Once-dormant limbs twitched in erratic spasms, their knuckles banging out a disharmonic tune.

Skin unthreaded from muscle, and muscle seeped from bone, the corpses deciding they wanted new shapes, or perhaps shapelessness. A shade of purple lived in them, as if their hearts now pumped psionic assaults through their blood vessels.

Except this was no illusion. Since before Alto's arrival in Pod L, something real had plunged its hands into the dead and meant to draw them close. Its earlier tremble had grown to a quake.

Alto broke from the railing and dragged Esme to her feet. She arose, as unresisting as the poorly anesthetized teenage girl glimpsed in her mind. The memory should have been off limits, the mind-hack forbidden. Esme deserved a thousand apologies, but not one would matter if she couldn't hear it.

"I'll take care of you," Alto said instead. Best they could do.

Esme's vacant eyes gave no answer, but she moved like Alto's shadow up the walkway. Zelany trailed at her side, likely stewing with some nonsensical comment about co-stars or new script material.

Alto glanced ahead to Pod K's malfunctioning doorway, where the Yellowjacket carried another two hundred and fifty corpses. No brain aliens in sight. They must have gone sneaking through the wraith-ports, and if they knew what Alto had done to the brain-beast, they would hide in those channels until Alto, Esme, and Zelany reached Pod F. Away from this nightmare.

The group had passed through the doorway into Pod

K, its walls echoing with gushing flesh, when Alto stalled. Damn, they'd left their hammer and harmonica on the walkway. Taken Esme, forgotten both weapon and music.

Alto left Esme's side to glance back, see if they could dash and snatch the harmonica before the blanket of corpses wove to the walkway. They glimpsed the hammer, not the harmonica.

And then a sight more skin-crawling than any mind-hack. Turning back had been a mistake, and now Alto would never unsee it.

The flood of corpses had already surged up Pod L's walls and formed horns around the walkway where it met the door to Pod M. The points merged in an archway above the wounded brain-beast. Dangling corpse-arms hovered useless toward its back as if it welcomed them. A creature that could hack a mind like a computer might hack flesh the same way.

Limp fingers stroked the brain-beast's pink-gray surface. A harsh twinge rocked its jelly glob body and brain-grown head, and then the quake spread through the looming corpse arch.

Each cadaverous head lifted on its stiff neck and leered toward Alto, their dead socket-sunken eyes yellowed and blackened and bruised and unseeing, and yet somehow seeing too. Bony jaws snapped open, revealing dark gums, cracked teeth, and lolling tongues. The brain-beast's mewling cry sang up their throats.

Alto retreated to Esme and Zelany, and they banged

across Pod K's walkway, but the cry chased them. The dead sang the brain-beast's cries in this cargo hold too.

And beyond, a far worse sound, a monotone feminine voice blasting through Zelany's interface:

Ten minutes until lockdown.

11

Pod K slid behind as Pod J opened.

Alto led the charge, mind and feet pounding out a *Pod F, Pod F* heartbeat rhythm every two steps. The wraith-plate slowed them down, more pain than weight, but they could manage. Esme ambled along behind them; Zelany snaked around her legs.

The workshop slipped around them, a blur of tools and wraith parts meant for maintenance. Alto could probably find a replacement hammer here if they had time to search, but they didn't know cabinet from closet-sized airlock on this pod. Jissika would usually sit at the squat desk or crouch over one scarred worktable or the other, her gloved hands busy replacing a faulty vertebra in a wraith's spine or tinkering with the connections between automated wires, all the while humming to herself, another amateur musician in the Yellowjacket's guts.

Plenty of wraiths lay broken throughout the ship, but no one worked on them here.

Zelany's screen beeped, interface overridden again: *Eight minutes until lockdown.*

Alto caught glimpses of dark shapes in the workshop's wraith-ports. The feral brains sat trembling like curled fists ready to throw a punch, but they held themselves back. Maybe they knew something worse followed.

Pod J gave way to Pod I.

The percussion of a thousand corpse-fists against starship walls chased through the closing door. Bulbous shuttle parts loomed on the walls, sheet metal siding, an engine replacement, every imaginable piece you would ever need to repair a shuttle. Enough to build a new one, given time. Alto and Esme had none.

Six minutes until lockdown.

The door opened to Pod H, a square space for physical recreation. A small auto-walk took up most of the floor, lift bars clung to the walls, and banded cords offered means to fight your own weight, all to stave off muscle deterioration during long space crossings. Clean as the wraiths had made its surfaces, they could not wash the human sweat stink from the air. Alto and Esme had to be adding to the eternal miasma. This recreation equipment would rattle once the wave of corpses pounded into Pod H.

Four minutes until lockdown.

Esme's hand was clammy. Alto glanced back to be

sure she wouldn't collapse. Her blank eyes seemed oblivious to the passing sections of the Yellowjacket, but her legs kept a clumsy half-sleeping shuffle, enough to keep moving. Her surgical memory suggested some accident years ago had ravaged parts of her skeleton, and her family must have had the money or credit to pay for augmentation procedures, no matter the unexpected trauma. The body mods might have stopped the feral brains from fully invading her mind, much like when Alto had met their first one in Pod Q.

But Esme had none of Alto's burdens or resistance. No Messenger in her head, but no wraith-node either.

Two minutes until lockdown.

They left Pod H behind and fled into Pod G. Restroom to one side; on the other, slender airlock doors met in a horizontal line of flat teeth in the wall. A round dining room formed the pod's center, and a combo cooking/clean-up station formed a semi-circle around it, divided by a slick countertop.

Past everything else stood the door to Pod F.

A white sheen cast Alto's hand in a shadow across rectangular dining tables. Zelany must have performed some kind of scan.

"Our friend's been recast into a bigger role," he said.

Alto didn't want to find out what that meant. Time to reach Pod F, no more stalling. They led Esme past the dining tables, around the semi-circle of sinks, heaters, and recycler ports.

Thirty seconds until lockdown.

Alto's shoulder jerked in its socket. They twisted in time to see Esme trip over the tail of another broken wraith and sprawl onto the floor. Her hand slipped from Alto's, and Alto stuttered a step away from her, toward the door to Pod F.

Fifteen seconds until lockdown. Fourteen.

The door called to Alto. They turned back to Esme.

Thirteen. Twelve. Eleven.

Alto scrambled onto the floor. "Esme, don't do this."

Ten. Nine. Eight.

One bare hand grabbed Esme's arm; the circuit-strewn left hand grabbed the other.

Seven. Six.

Alto dragged Esme's torso onto theirs and hauled her up. Grasped her hand. Led the way.

Five. Four. Three.

Rushed closer, heart racing, closer, chest squeezing, closer.

Two. One.

A sleek shutter crashed across Pod F's doorway and clamped into the floor with a heavy two-note clang.

"Not yet!" Alto shouted.

Lockdown initiated.

Three bars of yellow-and-black stripes ran from left to right across the shutter. Hazard warnings, as if Alto didn't know the ship was in danger. They slammed chest-first, wraith-plate against the shutter, and pounded their free fist. The shutter didn't care, and Alto's fist melted into a pleading hand, their palm flat against four inches of unyielding steel. Their eyes slid right and then left, demanding another door materialize. Restroom door to one side, airlock's split door to the other. No way to anywhere.

Emptiness, endlessness, and death, the Messenger had said.

Alto broke from Esme's hand, wheeled toward the cooking/clean-up station, and slammed both their fists on the countertop. Utensils jostled in the drawer underneath. Alto's heartrate went tectonic, ready to rattle both sternum and wraith-plate. If only it could shake the lockdown shutter open. Now what the hell were they supposed to do?

A corpse-driven cacophony rippled through Pod G. How far back was its source? Alto doubted the dead had remained a shapeless carpet of tissue, hair, and rotted fingernails. The brain-beast had drawn them up, hacking their flesh to reshape them the way the mind-hack had reshaped thoughts, and its new form pounded up the Yellowjacket pods.

"There's nowhere to go," Alto said, glancing to Esme. "We could really use your head right now."

Esme looked a million miles away. Maybe deep inside, parts of her mind were hard at work piecing her personality back together after Alto had cleaved it in two, but not fast enough to save anyone. Another apology seemed pointless, but Alto said it, meant it. If only they could reach inside and help Esme solve the puzzle.

Zelany slid behind the countertop and toward a sealed

wraith-port. "Been a good run, but the critics have spoken, and the owner's kicking us out of the theater."

"Not yet," Alto said. "There has to be a way."

Except there didn't. When did life entitle anyone to opportunity? Alto and Esme could stand here, and be absolutely fucked, and that might be their existence.

At least until the coming nightmare hit Pod G, and then Alto would miss these few dreadful moments caught between the sound of several hundred corpses and an unsympathetic shuttered door.

Zelany's narrow limbs prodded the wraith-port's edges. Ones and zeros danced down his interface screen and masked his Martian face until a switch ticked beneath his needle hands, and the wraith-port clacked open like a hungry mouth. He turned to Alto, his avatar grinning.

Alto studied the hole in the wall. A wraith couldn't override the full lockdown, but one could open the sealed wraith-ports and slip through. To cut them off would undermine Merchant Guild's counter-A.I. failsafe, in case the ship's A.I. had issued the lockdown against human will.

"This here's the road to stardom," Zelany said, jabbing the wraith-port. "Exit stage left, pursued by a bear. No way's that critic apt to fit."

"We won't fit either," Alto said.

"Might need to read from my script." Zelany's screen displayed a black mask, circuit arms, a wraith-plate, and a tail. "You're on your way already, champ."

Alto glanced over their augmentations. The first had

been by need and choice, but the others were defensive and dangerous considering Alto didn't own a single one. Each belonged to Merchant Guild, now fused to flesh. They owned every wraith, every corpse, the whole damn ship.

The ship. As a whole.

A terrible idea slid into Alto's head. They had been running up the pods one by one, headed for Pod F, ultimate goal of Pod A, facing feral brains, the brain-beast, the lockdown—all manner of problems stuffed inside the Yellowjacket.

But none of those problems could follow outside.

"A spacewalk to Pod A might work," Alto said, running a hand through their short hair. "Except we couldn't get back in."

"Pod A?" Zelany peeped. "I know that stage."

"We don't know if those brains are hiding in the channels." Alto shook their head.

Zelany shook his avatar's head too. "That's show biz, baby. Risks, remember?"

A jittery banging struck somewhere in Pod H, rattling the recreation equipment.

There was no other way. Alto grabbed Esme's hand again and led her toward the closet-sized airlock. Its thick doors slid into the floor and ceiling, and a red warning light flickered from above. Three black short-time spacesuits hung from the wall. Meant for quick repairs to pod connections, their back-mounted bubble packs held limited air, but enough to reach Pod A from here. Similar tech to the auto-detection in the wraith's hardware allowed the suits to contort to almost any body and limbs, albeit far gentler in doing so.

Alto tore open one suit, pressed it to Esme's front, and hit a switch at its neck. An electric pulse forced the rubbery black garment to splay around her, seeping under soles, clasping fingers and limbs and torso, and then a flick of the switch told the suit to contract. Alto then wrapped a suit around their own body. Its pliable material hugged every corner with fuzzy warmth, almost like a second skin. They sealed a bulbous white helmet over their head to lock in pressure and then sealed another over Esme's. Its inside smelled of cleaning chemicals, and Alto's surroundings now appeared muted behind a dark-tinted visor.

Around the corner from the airlock's doorway, the Pod G/Pod H door slid open in a storm of banging and mewling. Pod G jostled under oncoming girth. If the brain-beast had immersed itself in every corpse between the middle twin cargo holds, it would bring the weight of five hundred people into a single pod. If it had somehow drawn corpses from the rear pods at S and T, they would number a thousand. The Yellowjacket pod might fill floor to ceiling with dead flesh and hold together, but nothing within these walls would survive.

Zelany poised at the wraith-port, and a green hand flashed a thumbs-up beside his cartoon Martian face. "Break a leg," he said. He had to be wishing good luck in his program's strange way.

"You too," Alto said.

They watched Zelany dive into the wraith-port as the airlock's inner doors slid from floor and ceiling in clamping sets of teeth. The outer doors would soon fly open, exhaling Alto and Esme into the emptiness of space.

The dark. The Messenger scraped nails beneath Alto's mind.

A pale arm snapped through the inner doors' slender gap. Its hand didn't grope for Alto or Esme, only flopped useless in the airlock's flickering light. Not to hurt them; only to stall until the rest of its immense body thumped around the corner with enough strength to pry the doors open.

Alto clutched Esme's waist. "Hold tight," they said. Esme did nothing. That was fine; Alto had damaged her and she was their responsibility.

Fingers scraped unseen outside the airlock. Alto reached beside the remaining black spacesuit and yanked down a wall-mounted red lever. Grim yellow lights flashed across the ceiling, and then the airlock snapped open with another pair of teeth, this time over a dark celestial throat.

Angry wind rushed around the wedged arm, the vacuum of space sucking at it with the force of a starving universe. Alto didn't know if the brain-beast needed air to survive; the pressure change was all that mattered. A familiar feathery tingle lit their limbs as the Yellow-jacket's E-centric gravity gave way to the uncaring cosmos.

Sinew stretched gummy from the invading arm's bone, and then the limb tore loose. The inner doors clacked shut. If the brain-beast mewled in pain behind them, Alto couldn't hear anymore. They watched the ragged arm swirl free from the airlock and toward the stars. No more banging or reaching, nothing but another scrap of space debris gone silent outside the starship. The remaining black spacesuit swirled after it; Alto must have jimmied it loose in yanking the airlock's release lever. They pawed at the airlock's side and led Esme around an outer corner, where Alto clung to a metal rung jutting from the Yellowjacket's hull.

The airlock's teeth snapped shut, and Alto turned to watch the corpse arm drift. Already it had shrunken to a white fragment against countless distant lights, and the third spacesuit had vanished into the blackness.

A reminder that anything could disappear out there. Anyone. Even the smallest body might blanket the stars.

12

Forgetting the Yellowjacket's scale came easy from its insides. Cramped quarters and narrow halls pretended the starship was a long-buried tenement beneath some obscure planet's surface, the pressure of sediment and glacial ice squeezing the walls closer every journey between pods.

Turning from the empty eyes of the galaxy reminded Alto of the Yellowjacket's truth.

Its walls were armor on the outside. Twenty pods conjoined into a colossal segmented insect, seeking a planet around which to coil and lay its eggs. Metal rungs spined the starship's hide alongside grooves and shallow angles where hands and feet might catch if a spacewalker began to drift.

Alto squeezed Esme's hand and grasped the next rung from the airlock. And the next. Six segments to Pod A, and they were already nearing Pod G's edge. No gap separated the segments, only a line where pipes and tubes and doorways connected pod to pod.

"Easier than when people ran on the tops of trains in old Earth vids," Alto said, reaching Pod G's edge. "An adventure, nothing worse."

They realized they hadn't activated comms in Esme's helmet. She couldn't hear a word of reassurance.

Maybe that was for the best. Given time, Alto would only mumble out another string of useless apologies.

What had really happened to Esme? She'd recorded her message on the broken wraith in Pod O, with Praise shouting in the background, but then she should have run non-stop until she reached Pod F. She should have never reunited with Alto, let alone wandered behind them.

The brains must have got to her first. She might have been hiding in Pod O's halls, suffering a vicious mind-hack behind the water treatment pipes not ten feet from Alto the whole time her message played. And where was Praise? Dead in their room, or securing the rest of the crew in Pod A?

Alto could only hope everyone was safe.

The line between Pod G and Pod F slid under hand and foot, and Alto reached along the new line of rungs. Had Zelany crossed the wraith-port channels this far, or was he struggling to breach into Pod F? Maybe Alto should have told him to open the Pod F airlock instead.

Too late to change plans. Waiting outside Pod F's airlock would only mean letting Alto's and Esme's meager air supply dwindle while Zelany stood ready in Pod A. At most, Alto could try to ping Zelany's psionic nodes, but there would be no reading a wraith's signal in return. The Yellowjacket's hull cut them off from each other.

The only way forward would be to stick with the plan and reunite at the Yellowjacket's head.

Pod F gave way to Pod E. Alto saw no damage to the hull here; every rung remained firm. No scarring on the outside. If the brains had broken in, they must have done it elsewhere. More likely they had slipped in through some opening, maybe sneaking onto a shuttle from wherever the Star-Hopper had crashed as Alto had theorized before, but no planet reared its face from this side of the Yellowjacket. Its underside had to face the surface at an angle. If not for towing Esme, Alto would have crept along the hull to one edge or another and peered planetward. Maybe this planet was familiar.

Alto's gaze fixed on the outer darkness and its tiny points of light. A bluish cosmic cloud drifted what had to be millions of miles distant, but out here it looked close enough to sift suit-clad fingers through. Space could be beautiful despite all its threats. Alto wondered if the brain aliens came from this nearby planet or another one circling some distant star.

The blue-blackness of space sank into a bruised purple as a familiar voice scrabbled up Alto's thoughts.

"Here we are, in the dark," the Messenger said. "In the truest sense of me."

The wraith parts had held it off for a time, but now it had come clawing from the underside of Alto's mind. More wraith parts might quiet it again, but Alto had none at hand. They would need to endure the Messenger for now and drive new augmentations into flesh once reaching Pod A if it offered any spare wraith parts.

Before long, Alto might become a cyborg in earnest. The first living wraith in Merchant Guild history.

Pod E gave way to Pod D. Another water treatment center, the one everyone in the upper pods had to use now that they'd locked off Pod O and everything else behind Pod F. Would they notice Zelany's arrival via wraith-port and stop him? Hopefully he could prioritize the lives dangling outside the ship over the crew's pointless questions.

Alto gripped Esme's hand a little tighter and propelled them along the Yellowjacket's rungs toward Pod C. She followed, a weightless doll. With any luck, Praise had made it to Pod A and could shed some light on what had happened, maybe help snap Esme out of what Alto had done.

"She is in the dark," the Messenger whispered.

It crept along the starship on lithe limbs. No need for rungs when it had no genuine hands, no physical body. The muck had slithered off its skin since the cargo hold, replaced by a cloud of violet light. No face showed through the luminance, but stars seemed to dance in its short hair.

"If you were really out here, I couldn't hear you,"

112

Alto said. "And you couldn't hear me. You only exist where I go. Nothing outside my head."

"But within your head, I am the great nothing, the truest nothing." Closer now, the Messenger pawed alongside Alto, hands to Yellowjacket hull, as if the starship held a planet's gravity solely for this illusory creature. "I am the truth behind the universe."

Alto crossed onto Pod C's firm surface and tensed their mind. Zelany wouldn't understand a gentle psionic burst, but he might get a sense of Alto's and Esme's progress.

"From which inspiration mankind sowed the seeds of torment in the fertile perceptions of their terrible minds," the Messenger went on.

Alto looked ahead. Pod B. Pod A. Its airlock doors remained shut, but Zelany might be waiting until he noted someone outside the ship's head. Captain Day might stand beside him, along with the rest of the crew. Everyone waiting to welcome Alto and Esme, to tell them they were safe now, hush now, everything would be okay.

The Messenger scurried and spoke. "Now nurtured and grown into nightmare thoughts within the mindscape of emptiness, endlessness, and death."

Alto drew Esme onto Pod B. No focusing on the Messenger, only on traversing the rest of the Yellowjacket. From its head, they might even see the planet around which the starship orbited, where the Star-Hopper had crashed and drawn them.

The Messenger darted past Alto, over the line

between Pod B and Pod A. It perched above Pod A's airlock doors, hands between feet, head between bent knees, some grotesque violet-feathered bird against a bruised backdrop. A menacing figure, but it couldn't stop anyone. It could only taunt.

Alto took the rungs gently, one after another. No sense speeding too fast and flying past Pod A. Either the planet's gravity would then suck them down or the grandness of space would take them. Either way, an end. Alto hadn't led Esme this far to get them both killed now.

"I am your reflection," the Messenger said. "Forever dressed in the face of failure."

If only Alto could see that face.

They crossed the line from Pod B and slid at last over Pod A's airlock. The Yellowjacket's head stretched longer than its other pods, less a rounded container and more an arrow aimed at the stars. The same feisty yellowjacket as adorned the back of Alto's coat marked the hull, the starship's little mascot. Inside, Alto and Esme would find the meeting room, the Bridge, the cockpit, the captain's shuttle. Grid's core ran here, as did comms center, and engine control.

And they would hopefully find Captain Day, Co-Captain Ying, Praise, Jissika, Elvis, Dr. Calhoun, and maybe the Star-Hopper's crew too, anyone who'd survived. Maybe everyone.

Alto let go of Esme's hand, tucked an arm around her waist and pressed a palm to the airlock's sealed doors. Zelany had to know they were out here.

114

The airlock remained shut.

"Your death meets you," the Messenger said, craning its neck. "You have forsaken the Message for an end."

"It's not the end," Alto said.

They pawed along the airlock doors until their hand touched a panel. The lever inside would open an airlock under normal circumstances, but sliding it up and down now did nothing. The lockdown meant the airlock could only open from the inside.

Alto tensed their thoughts to Zelany and hoped he felt the psionic ping. A nudge. Anything.

Pod A lurched underfoot, and Alto grabbed a rung before the Yellowjacket could turn and abandon them. Doubtful the captain or Grid meant to shake off the tiny figures floating outside the airlock. The ship followed a preset course, a makeshift moon for the planet below.

As the orbit drew the Yellowjacket, the curved edge of the planet slid into view.

It was a maroon world of pockmarked soil. Not large judging by its circumference, maybe some other planet's former moon with enough ambition to strike out on its own. Black splotches marred its surface, too distant to tell whether they were ravines or bodies of water, but this did not look like a world thriving with life. No sign of foliage, fungi hills, colonies of any kind. A desolate place, good for dying.

Maybe that was why it had drawn the Star-Hopper and then the Yellowjacket. It needed lives so it could end them. Deaths to experience.

Static burbled into Alto's helmet. They turned to Esme, a blip of hope saying she might have come back to herself and activated her helmet's comms, but her face remained blank behind the dark sheen of her visor.

"Captain?" Alto asked, hoping for contact from within Pod A. "Praise? Jissika?"

The names quit as another starship hurtled overhead, its underside rushing only a few feet above Pod A's hull. The Yellowjacket was not alone in this planet's orbit.

Alto crushed themselves and Esme against the airlock doors. If one hull scraped the other, the Yellowjacket would spiral out of control. No human could withstand that titanic force, especially when clinging to a starship as it went careening toward a planet.

Esme squeezed close, spacesuit tight to spacesuit. Her mind was idle, but her body remembered comfort in this embrace.

"Please," Alto whispered. "Open."

"To beg the stars is the pinnacle of futility," the Messenger said. It stood from its perch above the shuttered airlock and spread its arms overhead as if beckoning the passing unknown starship. "These unfeeling specks of light cannot hold back the Message."

An arrow-shaped pod dragged a rounder pod, and another like it, and so on. Alto didn't count them, but guessed this was another segmented insect of a Merchant Guild vessel. No other faction designed their starships this way or required cute mascots on their vessels to convince people that the guild was their friend, like the wide-eyed squid marking one middle pod of the unnamed starship. Luminous Kingdom vessels would never, and Archon ships wore crimson and saffron slashes.

Static erupted again in Alto's helmet. "We can't control it!" a high-pitched voice shouted.

Alto tapped their helmet. "Anyone read me?" they asked. "This is Alto of the M.G. Yellowjacket. Get out of this space, or you'll hit us."

"The signal said—" Interference shushed the voice, a mouth fighting waves of rough audio. "Message—come through—do you hear?" Another static tide filled Alto's helmet, so loud that they reached to shut off comms.

A familiar voice paused their hand. Alto had only heard it back in their quarters through Zelany, but it had repeated enough to write itself into memory.

"Captain Afsar Sajid—Star-Hopper—handful of— immediate extraction—planet's surface—help, anyone."

The passing ship jerked as its tail-end slipped past the Yellowjacket's head, and the transmission cut out before it could repeat. Alto watched the squid-marked pod arc through space, hidden behind its ship's other segments, another insect lost out in this maroon world's orbit. This was not the Star-Hopper, stranded on the planet's surface, its crew awaiting extraction. This was a new ship, lured by the same distress call as the Yellowjacket and now suffering the same consequences.

"It is the Message," the Messenger said.

Alto doubted anyone aboard would luck into augmentations and psionic nodes. This crew's minds would falter under the mind-hack. Had they sent a shuttle down to the planet to rescue the Star-Hopper's crew? Maybe caught their own batch of feral brains? Alto couldn't tell, but the planet was the problem. Anyone who traveled here dove unknowingly into a cloud of chaos.

"And so the Message spreads," the Messenger said, lowering its arms.

Whatever that meant, the Messenger was right. The same fate would hit the next ship coming to the Star-Hopper's aid, and the next, on and on. This planet's skies would fill with ships from Merchant Guild, Luminous Kingdom, Archons, and other factions until someone finally marked it as a null site, at which point it would attract scrappers and scavengers. People would continue to die so long as the Star-Hopper pumped out its distress call.

There would be no extraction for their crew. No rescue for the Yellowjacket.

A two-note beeping began in Alto's helmet. Their air was running low. They and Esme should have drifted inside Pod A by now and torn off their helmets.

The air warning had to have hit Esme, too. She wouldn't understand the noise in her state, but the warning might shoot fresh panic through her mind. Had Alto not hurt her inside, she likely would have come up with a smarter plan to get them out of Pod G. Or she would have made sure they'd reached Pod F before the lockdown. If only the brain-beast hadn't messed her up one way. If only Alto hadn't messed her up another.

If, if, if. The possibilities never mattered. Reality stood undeterred.

"Let this death-sleep find you," the Messenger said, folding again into a perch. "Drift into the endlessness. It is your deserved punishment."

Alto leaned closer to Esme's helmet. "I'm sorry."

No recognition. No movement to say she'd somehow heard in the silence of space. The bad side of Alto's brain clawed at their thoughts. Maybe the brain-beast hadn't got into Esme's head at all. She might have genuinely realized their situation's hopelessness and chosen to spend her final moments in pleasure with Alto. Maybe she'd enjoyed their time back in quarters that much. She might even have admired Alto's rare confidence when standing bared to the world, or lying beneath her, or a thousand other ways Alto had taken for granted while lost in the inner snow of anxious thoughts, always cannibalizing their peaceful kin.

If Alto could just take a good thing for what it was.

"This terrible mind will not trouble you onward," the Messenger said, its head leaning deep over the airlock doors. "There is relief in death or relief in the Message. One way or the other, you will be free."

Alto tilted their head from Esme and glared up at the Messenger's indiscernible face. "Do you think you're fooling me?" Alto asked. "I know what you look like under the blood and clouds. Who you look like."

The Messenger lifted their head and cocked it like a predator sizing up prey. "I appear as you perceive me."

Alto only wanted the Messenger to disappear. Let the wayward crewmates of the M.G. Yellowjacket run out of air in peace. The others inside Pod A might still survive. That was all Alto could hope for anymore. Let the others get away and warn everyone to never come to this world.

The airlock trembled beneath Alto's body. Its doors slid open, another mouth in the Yellowjacket's side.

Alto grabbed a rung, hugged Esme close, and slung them both into the narrow airlock. Their bodies floated uncertain at its center, powerless without gravity, and then the doors shuddered close. Invisible hands groped up Alto's legs, their body, and then slammed them against the floor. Esme landed rough beside them.

Inner doors creaked open in a rush of oncoming air. Alto tore off their helmet, then crawled toward Esme and did the same for hers. The air had almost run out. Not as close as it could have been, but closer than Alto had ever wanted.

Past the airlock's inner doorway, Zelany collapsed from the wall. His right arm hung twisted in a limp corkscrew, and a crack ran down the side of his black mask. The green cartoon face on his screen twitched in and out of a clear signal.

His voice came warped and stilted. "Tough. Crowd."

13

Beyond Zelany, Pod A's meeting room offered a friendlier emptiness than the rest of the Yellowjacket. No people, but no monsters either.

It told an unclear story instead. The central long table stretched between immovable floor-mounted seating, the furniture mapped by dark brown puddles and a scattering of stained papers. To the airlock's left stood the door to the Bridge. Past the table, the restroom. To the right, the door to Pod B, which held quarters for Captain Day and Co-Captain Ying.

Two wraith-ports glistened to either side of that door, one sealed shut, the other a gaping dark hole with its rim rattling. Feral brains had to be sliding nearer to finish what they'd started on Zelany.

"Get behind us," Alto said, waving Zelany back. "You're safe with me."

The Messenger's voice floated through Pod A. "Is anyone?"

A mewling crying slid from the open wraith-port and cut down Alto's spine. That noise couldn't be the brain-beast. Its thundering mass could never fit through the cross-pod channels.

"You're wrong, Alto," the Messenger seemed to sing. Nowhere in sight, but forever close, anchored in Alto's mind. "You're always wrong, and everyone's too nice to tell you the truth."

Alto opened their mouth to answer, but the wraith-port trembled again. They turned toward it as the first globs of pink-gray corpse paste surged into Pod A. Bony limbs jittered across its surface like insects stuck in greedy mud. The puddle clawed over the floor, up the wall, and reached the ceiling. A head-sized brain sprouted from the pink muck, stretching from a lengthy neck rimmed by rib bones and maroon muscle. The brain-beast had joined with the Yellowjacket's cargo, and now oxygen somehow flowed through once-dead tissue, the flesh a form of paper with the flesh-hack for its pen.

Zelany crawled toward Alto's feet. "Crowd too fast, couldn't lock the theater doors behind." His avatar's mouth popped open again, but only static fizzed through this time. Alto didn't know how to help him.

Or Esme. She grasped her head in both hands and then thrashed at her spacesuit, triggering its release and letting it drape from her body. The vacant daze snapped out of her eyes.

"It wants me," she said, almost astonished. "It wants to know me."

Pod A was a dead end, nowhere left to run. Only the Bridge offered hope of a hidden crew who might have a better plan.

Alto grabbed for Esme's arm, and then Zelany's, and pulled them toward the Yellowjacket's head. Esme only stumbled. Zelany sagged corpselike, tail twitching beneath him. A tongue of purple static licked Alto's eyes, some attempted mind-hack, maybe successful against Esme.

Not Alto, never again. They turned to the brain-beast and tensed their thoughts.

Corpse limbs spilled from the wraith-port, their knuckles back to banging an endless discordant rhythm. The brain-beast let them rattle and hang as it bellyflopped forward on the sea of pinkish slime, the only way it knew how to move even when joined by a mountain of muscle and bone.

A lithe figure cloaked in violet light rode the beast's back.

"This one knows the Message," the Messenger said, triumphant now. "And the Message knows them, too."

Alto gritted their teeth and thrust their mind toward the brain-beast. It had known the cathedral of gore, same as the feral brains, and it would break like last time.

A bulbous limb of corpse parts slashed across the meeting room table, catching papers as it rammed into Alto's chest. The blow knocked them back, and dead people's fingernails and jutting bones shredded the black spacesuit open over Alto's wraith-plate and coat.

The brain-beast had lost interest in mind-hacks. A product of a flesh-hack, it had come hunting for blood.

Another pink-gray pseudopod snapped from the growing flesh balloon and crashed toward Alto. They dodged back against panicked Esme, and a limb of sinew-fused skulls cracked against the hard floor.

"To act is to fail," the Messenger said. It skittered across the brain-beast and aimed a narrow limb at Esme. "You knew this truth before meeting her, and you will know it again when she is gone."

Alto braced a protective left arm across Esme's chest. Her fists clenched tight at Alto's muscle, but they couldn't feel it. The wraith circuitry must have numbed their nerves.

"My skin hurts," Esme said. She gave a chest-deep groan and then buckled over Alto's arm. "It wants me."

The brain-beast's snakish neck curved now, aiming at Esme. Wrinkles flexed down its front, squeezing a dry-throated, cracking scream up Esme's throat. Alto pressed her back; they needed to go, right now, haul themselves into the Bridge, escape this nightmare for even a few more minutes. Esme leaned to follow.

But her skin tugged toward the brain-beast like oversized clothing caught in a door, and she belted out a skinned-alive scream.

Alto let go of her, and she dropped quivering to her hands and knees. Corpse limbs dangled toward her, same

124

as they'd reached for the brain-beast in Pod L.

A flesh-hack in progress. Alto hadn't realized these things had that kind of power over living people, but if the brain-beast could draw up half a thousand corpses from the depths of the Yellowjacket's middle cargo holds, why not the flesh from one frightened crewmate?

Was that why no one else stood here in the meeting room? The blood-spattered table told part of a story, and the brain-beast's corpse flood might tell another. Alto and Esme might be the Yellowjacket's only surviving crew.

Alto reached out, flinched back, reached again. Maybe everyone else was dead, but Alto couldn't let the brain-beast have Esme too.

Pink muck swelled over both wraith-ports and the Pod B door. Soon it would coat the table, fill the restroom, and ooze all the way through the Yellowjacket's head. Esme began to slide as if dragged by some unseen force, and her palms squeaked against the floor.

"No, no, it's taking me!" she shouted.

Alto scrambled at her ankles. Better to risk wounding her in breaking a flesh-hack than surrender her to this monstrous living tomb.

"She will know the Message," the Messenger said, dancing down the brain-beast's side. "And the Message will know her."

Alto wanted to argue, had nothing. They grasped at Esme's legs.

The brain-beast's pull was stronger. Corpse limbs reached through the Messenger's light and draped across

Esme. She twisted and flailed, turning her back on the pinkish wall, her eyes to Alto.

The dead didn't care. Their fingers wanted her, would join her to the brain-beast's flesh-hack. Her blouse peeled open from the shoulders, splaying layers of skin and tissue. Scarlet tubes slashed from the pinkish tide and drove into the muscle around her spine.

Alto hugged both arms around Esme's middle. Her skin wrinkled over either hand, ready to slide off, and her chest pressed Alto's cold wraith-plate.

Rage filled her eyes. She curled one hand into a hooked claw and scratched down Alto's neck and sternum. Purple nails cracked against the wraith-plate's rim. Another hand smacked Alto's side, palm against wraith-plate's clutching limbs. She fought like she didn't want to be free. The brain-beast must have hacked her mind to soften her into its flesh.

"I don't want to go without you," Alto said. They glanced back to Zelany. "Get to the Bridge, see if anyone's alive to help us."

Zelany pawed his working arm at the floor and then curled his tail against his wraith-plate. His avatar flitted over his screen.

Corpse limbs climbed Esme's shoulders and kissed Alto's skin with cold and clammy fingertips. They would spread the flesh-hack from one survivor to another.

"To know the Message," the Messenger said, pacing at Alto's side.

Could Esme be helped? Had she even snapped out of

that daze, or was her new violence the work of the brain-beast, nothing more?

Alto knew too little. Maybe that had always been the case, in every scenario across their disastrous life. They tensed their thoughts past Esme, toward the monster. Neither of them would become part of the flesh-hack if Alto could help it.

Even if it killed them.

Esme's chipped claws softened to grasping hands at Alto's shoulders. The anger in her eyes melted to desperation, eager to speak above her silent lips.

"I wish I could make it better for you," Alto said. "I really do."

Esme's voice crawled up, stiff and dry but hers. "You can."

Her skin trembled as if sucking toward the brain-beast. Corpse limbs reached past her and tugged open Alto's shredded spacesuit with dead fingers. Their nails carved Alto's coat and clothes and skin. They craved this flesh, desperate to draw every possible body into the brain-beast's unity.

Alto tried to back away as tatters fell from bloodied naked skin. They couldn't escape, Esme clinging like Alto was the last rung on the Yellowjacket to save her from flying off into nothingness. She lunged up Alto's body and pressed lips to lips, wanting this flesh for one reason while the dead wanted it for another. Between each, they'd tear Alto apart.

The moment would kill everyone, and its heaviness

sank Alto into the kiss. They could let Esme have this one distraction. Let themselves have it, too.

A sensual quake worked across their nerves and spread through Esme, up her spinal tubes, into the brain-beast's pink-gray flood. Corpse limbs drooped from Esme's shoulders and into the fleshy muck, fingers twitching but unneedy. The beast's rib-coated neck stilled, and the brain settled as if staring in awe. An almost placated beast, same as the feral brains had sat unmoving between cargo holds when Alto and Esme last clung to each other

But why?

Esme pressed deeper into Alto, fingering the ragged claw marks in their skin, the remaining scraps of clothing. Warmth flooded Alto's body, their mind, as if kissing and touching and being touched could cleanse the mindscape of inner snow, psionic intrusions, the Messenger, all of it.

A secret here—distraction in this rush of chemicals. Some shifting balance inside had tripped up the aliens.

Had Esme known when she'd approached Alto back in Pod L, or was that too much to hope? She might have been suffering a mind-hack, disorientation, anything, but deep down, she might have figured a way out. The same pleasure they'd drifted into before this catastrophe began could cloud their thoughts and busy their bodies, blocking mind-hack and flesh-hack alike.

Brilliant, beautiful Esme. If this had been her intent all along, then she'd found a path forward.

And had Alto let this intimacy take them in Pod L,

forgotten the lockdown, immersed mind and body in what they would have rather done with Esme than face the Yellowjacket's life-and-death threats, they might not have needed to race the lockdown at all. They might not have lashed out at Esme, mistaking her for psionic illusion. No daze, no fugue state. Instead, she might have reminded Alto what she'd already taught them in sessions. Always the damn brain was to blame.

A voice whispered in Alto's ear. "And you're letting it happen now," the Messenger said. "How would you put it? Another Perfect Alto Fuck-Up."

Esme jerked from Alto's chest and fell backward onto the floor. Her eyes and mouth popped wide, and skin flayed from her arms and sides as corpse limbs encircled her again.

"Wait," Alto coughed. Free to move again, they grabbed at Esme's ankle, her wrist, anything. "We can push them off. We can distract each other."

Esme slid beneath the brain-beast's shadow. Nothing she did would matter here. This was Alto's fault. Even undressed and melting into Esme's arms, Alto had let inner snow and anxious thoughts poison another moment, and this time Esme was too weak the stop it.

"You cannot help her," the Messenger said, still at Alto's ear. "Helpful is not what you are."

Alto reached for Esme again, but the brain-beast's corpse-thick limbs sent Alto skittering back into Zelany.

Away from Esme. Too late to help her.

The small of her back sank into the pink-gray flesh

mound, where the brain-beast's curling neck crossed over her, almost possessive. Her face paled, her torso leaned forward, and a wet scream croaked up her throat.

"It's the—" she started, her mouth spraying red phlegm. "It's the Message!"

Alto froze. Where the hell had Esme heard that?

She said nothing else. Her shoulders bubbled until the skin tore, baring a vaster span of muscle down her back, where the brain-beast's tubes danced a death jig. Her face sank in wet ribbons as her arms flopped limp to either side. A vicious quake rattled her body, an egg ready to hatch, and then the bones and meat of her torso sloughed into her lap.

Alto threw their arms across their screaming face, hands splayed, couldn't see this, couldn't stop seeing it, not if they wanted to save Esme.

As if anyone remained to be saved.

Esme's quivering husk dribbled to the floor in a stew of once-human pieces. Its surface slid around her legs and curved toward the brain-beast to join its girthsome body. Bones split through her chest, cracked along her spine, freeing their caged organs as a dark lump swelled from her back upon a tangle of entrails. Deep wrinkles carved its pink-gray surface. A nest of snaking tubes wriggled from its underside, pulling the dark lump free from its birthing shell.

No eyes, no face, no features. A brain the size of Alto's chest, same as they'd seen when this nightmare began.

Alto stumbled backward, gasping for another elusive scream. The new feral brain wriggled in place, maybe to gets its bearings, and then it slid inches closer. *She* slid inches closer? Alto didn't know; the feral brain blurred under fresh tears.

One retreating foot scraped Zelany's spiny tail. A painful twinge shot across Alto's mind—couldn't collapse, couldn't give up, had to get away. They turned to Zelany and hauled him up by the torso. They needed to reach the Bridge. Nothing had changed.

And yet everything had changed. Wet tubes played a strange tune as they slapped the floor. A purple sheen wreathed the edges of Alto's eyes—new feral brain, new mind-hack—but why bother after the sight of its birth. Or was it Esme's death? Her transformation?

Alto had misunderstood every step of surviving this nightmare. Failure to learn from Esme, failure to reach Pod F, even failure in the beginning when they'd wondered where the rest of the crew had gone and where the feral brains had come from. Failure to tie those two mysteries together in one clear answer.

There were no aliens on the Yellowjacket. Never had been.

14

Alto blinked away tears as the Bridge door opened. With no way to stop the brain-beast, few options remained at the ship's dead end.

Zelany was quiet and heavy in Alto's arms, and his weight felt like cradling a child. His tail coiled against Alto's wraith-plate, and steel tapped steel at each panicked step. Blackness filled his screen, but a low hum ebbed out as the Bridge door shut behind Alto, as if the skull underneath Zelany's black mask wanted to speak. His processors seemed desperate to connect with his wraith-nodes.

Alto wanted to say everything would be okay, but they didn't know how that might be. Finding Jissika alive would be a miracle.

But then, wasn't everyone alive in different shapes? Even Esme?

Alto stepped deeper into the Bridge and realized their tears would have been a comfort. Better to see this ruin through a watery veil or not at all.

Two pale yellow circles marked the dark floor's center where one shaft descended to engine control and the other to the captain's shuttle. From those hatch doors, the Bridge forked in three to the comms center control panel, the two-seater cockpit looking toward a curved forward-facing window, and Grid's main terminal, a tremendous screen built into the wall and surrounded by wire-filled panels.

Blood painted splotchy patterns across every surface, and a coppery stink filled the air.

Alto's muscles softened as their knees bent, but they forced themselves to keep standing. No wallowing in the tatters of skin, clothes, and hair dotting the floor. Everyone here had burst open long before Alto's arrival. Crying for the crew wouldn't turn them back into people.

Grid's screen stood dark. One wall panel hung open beside it, decorated in rubber tendrils. An antique leather toolbelt lay twisted on the floor beneath. Its tools were smaller and more specialized than those Alto had thrown to the dead or left behind on Pod L's walkway along with their harmonica. These were meant for fixing malfunctioning wraith servos when they wouldn't automatically connect, or for replacing a damaged part.

Jissika's tools. No one who'd gathered at the Bridge must have known where to find Elvis for fixing the terminal. Hell, maybe he'd been the one to break Grid after turning into another feral brain. Jissika must've been trying repairs as best she could. She knew wraiths, and they were practically Grid's limbs. The thought process made sense. She might even have put Grid in order eventually had she not run out of time.

But then the Message had torn through her, and scabby black puddles mixed with bits of moist bone told the rest.

If Grid hadn't been sabotaged before, Jissika's mid-repair transformation had ravaged it beyond repair, its wires severed while gory chunks of once-human melted inside its processor. That might have been the goal, supposing the brains understood their mysterious Message at all.

A gentle voice followed into the Bridge. "The Message is not understood," the Messenger said. "To have it is to know it, and to know it is to know the dark."

Alto bit their lip not to answer; they would not feed the Messenger. They had bigger problems, like how much longer the automated life support systems of air, heat, water, and gravity would last without A.I. and wraith maintenance.

Doubtful Alto would survive to see those troubles come to fruition. Any minute now, the brain-beast would surge onto the Bridge in a gushing flood. Esme, too, in her new form. No human's brain sat that large in their skull; the rest of her muscle must have repurposed itself—or been repurposed by the Message.

"There, you are so close to knowing," the Messenger

said, slinking through the empty Bridge.

Its quiet footsteps pretended the crew hadn't left puddles across the floor, the mess being all that remained of Jissika, Captain Day, Co-Captain Ying, and Dr. Calhoun. Maybe Elvis and Praise, too, though they'd likely transformed elsewhere on the ship judging by circumstances. Everyone was gone, their human tissue and skull fragments crushed across the Bridge, down the ship, wherever the Message had found them. Feral brains now, repurposed like their cargo. If the brain-beast had absorbed them along with the corpses, there would be no way to tell who'd been dead or who'd been alive when the Yellowjacket's journey began.

What if their new brain forms had never intended the mind-hack? Esme had to be scared after her transformation. Anyone would be. The other brains, too. They might only have been trying to communicate with Alto, but their minds were no longer compatible. A misunderstood greeting might have malformed into a nightmare.

That feral brain Alto had beaten with a hammer at Pod P—who had it been? Praise or someone else? There was no way to know. No one left to rescue.

Only Alto. The rest of the crew must not have had any augmentations to stall the mind-hack, and even if they had, that wouldn't have stopped the flesh-hack. Alto's stolen nodes alone had saved them, along with wires in their brain and machines across their body.

Except since the crew had become the feral brains, the

cause of the mind-hack and flesh-hack, what had hacked them in the first place? The psionic disease had run rampant down the Yellowjacket, first disorienting the crew and then transforming them.

Where had they caught it from?

The Messenger paced between the comms center and Grid, its figure distorting in fits of purple static. Esme hadn't noted anyone else besides Alto in Pod A minutes ago, but she'd mentioned the Message. Was the Messenger a unique symptom of the same psionic disease, solely for Alto? Or maybe the way it presented itself was more their problem, as a reflection in form, the anxious thoughts, a mouthpiece for the bad side of Alto's brain. This monster might have come to the others as a friendly face, or a voiceless sensation, and who would kill the Messenger? It only wanted to deliver its Message.

Bones rattled outside the Bridge's sliding door. A behemoth of corpses filled the meeting room, and soon it would fill the cockpit with flesh putty. Alto imagined tubes and fingers slopping closer. Esme would slip inside ahead of the brain-beast, desperate for a strange new kiss.

Alto set Zelany down beside the Messenger, rushed toward Grid to grab Jissika's sticky toolbelt, and then hauled back and opened one of the floor hatches. A short ladder-mounted hole descended into a white chamber. Alto hugged Zelany close and began down the rungs.

The Bridge door slid open as Alto's head sank beneath the hatchway. A mewling cry rang over wet slopping sounds and the rattle of jittering limbs.

Alto snapped the hatch shut overhead and then followed the ladder one-handed, rung by rung, until they dropped through the roof port of Captain Day's small shuttle. One fist pounded a button beside the ceiling port as something beat against the hatch atop the ladder. Doubtful the brain-beast would figure out how to open it, but no point waiting to find out. Alto had been wrong about everything else up until now, after all.

The shuttle carried little more than a few rations of nutrient brick, some potable water, a spacesuit and helmet, and enough oxygen for thirty conscious hours. Cooling the vessel might slow an occupant's heartrate and breath to stretch those supplies, but Alto didn't know the math.

They only knew it was time to go.

15

The shuttle was a cramped arrow of sleek white surfaces broken up by supply cabinets. Its dark cockpit seat awaited behind a panel of buttons, switches, and two terminals, the higher screen to display what lay ahead of the shuttle, the lower to display the shuttle's general health. No Grid here, or any other A.I., only automatic systems and the poor wraith cradled against a scavenged wraith-plate.

Alto would have to fly the shuttle on their own. They settled into the captain's seat and ticked half a dozen labeled switches.

Zelany stirred in their arms. Nothing blinked across his screen, but his tail coiled tight around Alto's right arm, pricking the skin, an infant's frail fist grasping a nearby finger.

Maybe Zelany needed that comfort and closeness, and

a little tenderness too. Merchant Guild might have said wraiths were machines using the layout of human nerves and brain for better functionality. Maybe Alto was projecting their loneliness and desperation onto an undead cyborg.

But deeper than that, they could believe somewhere between Zelany's programming and his corpse frame that he remembered his old life and the fear of death possessed by all the universe's creatures.

Never mind that some part of him had already died. Merchant Guild acted as if they simply fitted computers onto the dead, but the neural pathways for wires suggested elements of life lingered. Otherwise, what was the point? Some piece of humanity must remain to let the wraiths become Merchant Guild's failsafe against rogue shipboard computers. A ghost of a person haunted these machines.

It wasn't right. No one trusted a shipboard A.I. to work alone after the L.K. Cassandra, but maybe the work shouldn't have been left to humans either. Maybe mankind should have held off on traveling the stars until they first fixed their relationship with themselves and the things they made.

The shuttle screens lit up, the lower with meters and numbers, the upper with a down-facing crescent of black space and starlight where the cosmos hugged a maroon planet. A blinking display showed the shuttle had pinged the Yellowjacket for release. Other shuttles needed permission from authority, but the captain's personal vessel overrode that necessity. Besides, Alto was the last remaining crewmate of the Yellowjacket. Authority fell to them.

"Or are the others alive up there?" The Messenger crouched behind Alto's seat, a violet demon at their back. "In their new knowledge and form, do they not still have authority? Are you a survivor, or a mutineer?"

Alto tapped at the lower screen. Every surface hummed with motion as the shuttle floated loose from the Yellowjacket's underside. Alto let it drift into the planet's orbit until the pointed front of Pod A joined the display screen.

They then began to steer away from the planet. The best course would be to speed out of its gravity field, away from mind-hacks and feral brains and everything else, and hope someone plucked the shuttle up from open space. Alto would worry over how to explain their new augmentations and the Yellowjacket's fate if they lived long enough to meet another living human.

"You have chosen the emptiness and the endless-ness." The Messenger crept to Alto's side and peered at the star-dotted upper screen. A smile lit through glowing skin. "You have chosen death."

"Maybe," Alto said, fighting back fresh tears. "But I'll die far away."

The Messenger's face turned in slow inches toward Alto, and its smile widened. "But never far enough. I am the dark, and the dark is vast." Glowing eyes blinked back to the cosmos. "Wherever you choose to die out there,

140

you will come to me."

Alto steered the shuttle until it faced only the outer blackness. They refused to believe this parasite was some cosmic presence. It was nothing more than a voice in Alto's head, birthed between clashing psionic tethers, maybe through the feral brains, if not at their source. Out there, maybe Alto could escape it.

A red square blinked in the corner of the shuttle's lower screen, a warning of oncoming debris. They would wait for it to pass, let the Yellowjacket and the planet take the brunt before the shuttle charged into the open. Whether Alto lived or died, their vessel was in for a long and difficult journey.

Chunks of debris crossed the stars within the shuttle's upper display in tremendous glimmering fragments. Smaller pieces flew in familiar shapes—seating, pipework, sheets of pod walls. One ruined scrap of hull flashed a wide-eyed squid.

The starship Alto had seen during their spacewalk with Esme. Its pieces scattered wide, each remnant falling planetward. The ship must have collided with another, maybe even the tail end of the Yellowjacket. If the planet had a thin atmosphere, it might let these fragments pass right through to cut and scar the surface anew. Little chance they might crash into the Star-Hopper and shatter it beyond recognition. If they did, they would end the distress call that had drawn the Yellowjacket and anyone else here, and then the eventual parade of future doomed starships would never come.

"It is endless," the Messenger said. "There is no stopping the Message."

Its lithe limbs held rigid, so different from the wild squirming of the feral brains and brain-beast and Esme. She had died with the Message on her lips, meaning she'd heard that word somewhere in relation to this disaster. A version of the Messenger in her head must have told her.

If everyone on the crew had seen this thing, filtered through their maybe-healthier minds, it had to come from somewhere, same as the rest of the psionic junk. Maybe the same source as the mind-hacks, the feral brains.

The Message.

Alto rubbed their double-noded forehead. "You don't live inside me."

The Messenger stared into Alto, lips pursed.

"There's nowhere in my head," Alto said. "No *there* for you to live. My mind's a network of thoughts and memories, and maybe your friends tricked me into opening a door inside, and maybe it's my fault you look like me, talk like my brain when it hates me, but you're coming from somewhere else. There's no Messenger without the Message. So, what's the Message?"

Alto waited for a response. If the Messenger mimicked the bad side of Alto's brain, it had to have something to say.

Zelany's interface lit in Alto's lap. A neutral feminine voice rang from his mask, similar to the lockdown warning before: *Emergency linkage, limited functionality, please stand by.*

142

"The show must go on," Zelany said. No green cartoon Martian face blipped the mask, but the voice was his, light and boyish and enthusiastic.

Alto leaned in and hugged him, clinking their wraith-plates together. "You scared me. Thought I'd be on my own."

White dots flitted over Zelany's screen. His voice began, "It's a risky—"

The neutral voice took over again. *Upgrade incompatible. Please perform maintenance or wraith unit may cease functionality.*

Alto fumbled beside the cockpit seat for Jissika's blood-spattered toolbelt. Helplessness jellied their limbs; these were unfamiliar tools. Some were the usual screwdrivers of various sizes, but others—what was this tiny hook for? Why did one small cylinder hold a crystal on the end? For psionics? A strange kind of wrench might have removed and reattached wraith-tail vertebrae, but Zelany's didn't seem damaged, and Alto had no spare parts. His tail coiled farther up Alto's arm in a snug embrace.

Zelany's voice popped through his mask. "An encore? For me? Never thought I'd see the day."

"Jissika was the specialist." Alto's throat tightened. "I don't know how to fix you."

A quiet settled over Zelany. His tail's grip tightened. "Stardom was never my thing, champ. Management, directing, the backstage. I point the spotlight, never standing in it. But lift a few lines from my script, you get

143

me?"

Alto glanced over Zelany's mangled arm, scuffed wraith-plate, and the glowing nodes on his black mask.

That damn neutral tone shot in, uncaring, unfeeling. *Shutdown imminent. Please perform maintenance.* As if it blamed Alto. Maybe it was right to do so.

Zelany's tail squeezed so tight, it made Alto's arm ache. "Don't let them rotten tomatoes and hecklers and cheap seat-sitting gum-chewers get you down. I know—" Static crackled under his mask. "I know a star when I see one."

Alto pressed their arms tight around Zelany's trunk. Useless Alto. Pointless Alto. The Messenger had been right. Another Perfect Alto Fuck-Up.

"Sometimes it's a solo act," Zelany went on. "That's show biz, baby." His intact arm twisted in place, opening a space within the circuits and wires, and a narrow lump fell into Alto's lap. It bore a synth-wood comb and brass reed plates.

Alto's harmonica. No wonder they'd missed it when crossing the Yellowjacket's cargo holds. Zelany must have grabbed it after Alto had slung their toolbelt at the Messenger, before they'd all fled the rising wave of dead. Alto plucked it up in one hand and stared into Zelany's mask.

The screen flashed a winking green face, shuddering beneath endless static snow. "Knock 'em dead," Zelany said, wraith-nodes glowing bright. "I know you can."

Emergency linkage exhausted. Shutting down.

Zelany's interface snapped to darkness. Face gone, lights gone, only a black mask with a skull beneath it.

Alto gritted their teeth, bit their tongue, and fought the shaking in their limbs. They had lost every fight since they'd stepped into Pod L's cargo hold; why not one more? Heavy breath sagged through their lips at the edge of another ragged sob.

Their breath flowed into the harmonica and whistled the slightest note. A little music in an empty shuttle.

Alto lifted the harmonica in both hands, one arm still coiled in Zelany's tail, the other fitted with undead circuitry, and began to play. The notes came slow and warped at first, but then they smoothed into whatever melody came thoughtlessly through Alto's lips. It was the nameless kind of song they'd played for Esme, and perhaps now they played it for Esme again, and Zelany, and everyone lost aboard the Yellowjacket.

Against this despair, only a nameless song would do.

The last note sang through the brass reed plates as Alto remembered the figure sitting to their left. They turned to a face of glowing violet.

"You are no more alone than you were before," the Messenger said, and it placed a hand beside Zelany's mask. "This was not a soul."

The Messenger didn't understand. It was an avatar of cruel thoughts. Love didn't factor in.

Time to amputate it from Alto's mind, at least for a while. They would accept Zelany's invitation, with humility and gratitude. Alto set down their harmonica and tripped a chunk of circuitry from Zelany's intact arm.

"The falsehood will haunt your thoughts," the Messenger went on, but its voice weakened as the circuits dug into Alto's naked leg. "You will want someone, pretend they've come to you."

Alto plucked at the wire over Zelany's mask and stripped his wraith-nodes loose. Wraiths only ever carried three. How would a human mind make out with five? Alto jammed one node in, no hesitation this time at the electronic *ping*, and welcomed its icy pain like an old friend.

"You will think someone stands around the corner." The Messenger's voice sank to a whisper. "Look, and you will see no one. Emptiness beckons."

Alto didn't wait for the new augmentation's pain to finish; best to get it all done. They jammed the last two psionic nodes between the others, forming a line of five from temple to temple.

"But you are not alone," the Messenger said, fading. "I am here."

The wraith-nodes' drills did not cancel each other out; agony crossed Alto's skull, into deep places, purpling their mind and stretching their thoughts as if a skinless adult wanted to wear a child's hide. Too little, spread too thin. Alto squeezed the cockpit seat's arms and screeched, their sounds barely human.

The Messenger cut through, its voice soaked in violet. "I promise, it is dark here," it said. "And the dark is all you will know."

"I'm going to find out what you really are," Alto said through gritted teeth. "And then you're going to wish you'd left me alone."

The icy pain snapped away, and merciful peace followed. Alto sank into their seat. Sweat coated their skin, and they panted for breath. A curious finger stroked their forehead—five nodes. Would it be enough for where Alto meant to go?

Stripping Zelany of further pieces felt like disrespecting who he'd been, maybe acting out a flesh-hack itself. Still, he had offered, and Alto needed more. They could only whisper apologies and gratitude as they tested Jissika's tools, found the right one, and pried the wraith-tail from Zelany's torso.

Made of steel and some other alloy, spined by vertebrae, and longer than Alto's leg, the prehensile tail looked like it might do some damage if wielded by anyone but a harmless wraith. Circuits and wires jutted from its stump, waiting to be plugged into another torso.

Alto instead cut one of Jissika's tools into their right forearm and jammed the stump into flesh. Its pieces whirred in confusion, but it wasn't like a wraith's torso had active muscles to tell a tail what to do. All it needed for functioning was its servos, internal power source, and a set of artificial nerves.

Or real ones.

Alto's world sank again into agony. Their arm twitched as merciless wires corkscrewed across bone and meshed with muscle. Alto's spine quaked in a melted-flesh inferno. They might have screamed for it to stop, and then screamed they were sorry, though they weren't sure to whom, but they could only half-remember as they swept in and out of consciousness.

They woke to the shuttle thudding against the Yellowjacket's underside. A display light warned of a collision, no damage reported. Alto muttered another, "Sorry." Probably to their body, which was theirs and yet abused like never before, or maybe to Zelany and Esme again.

Maybe to the shuttle. It deserved every possible apology for where Alto would steer it next.

A maroon curve haunted the upper screen's edge. This was the world where the Star-Hopper had crashed. Where its distress call had shot out into space and drawn the Yellowjacket, the ship with a squid on its hull, and more to come if they weren't already on their way, following interplanetary faction protocols of various kinds. The trouble had started in that desolate hell.

It would end there, too.

Alto laid a reluctant hand on the control panel, gave the stars a longing glance, and then steered the shuttle toward the unknown maroon planet. Their aching right arm weighed heavier with the wraith-tail, but they had some experience with it coiling there while Zelany had curled here shutting down. Dying. Alto could manage lifting it now that they'd taken that piece, enough to tick the shuttle's communications awake to lead them to the Star-Hopper.

A familiar distress call filled the cramped cockpit. Captain Afsar Sajid. Star-Hopper. Immediate extraction. Alto doubted there was anyone left to rescue besides the countless future souls who might drift toward this world.

That was fine. Life did not keep secret that if you planned to stand up and do the right thing, you should always plan to do it alone. The universe made no promises anyone would stand with you.

But Alto would stand nonetheless. If they couldn't escape, then they would make sure no one else died here.

And if they couldn't have life, they would at least take a chance on revenge.

THE MESSAGE

16

Alto switched off comms a few minutes before the shuttle jerked to a rough landing in a shallow maroon valley. No more need for the distress call. They had arrived.

A soft rhythm tapped the shuttle's roof. Rain or sediment? Maybe pieces of the other starship burning up on entry after all. Alto sat back and listened, but soon the thought of precipitation reminded them too much of inner snow. That anxious symptom should have left them alone since corpses had torn off Alto's clothes, but bodily love had collapsed since watching the brain-beast husk Esme's flesh from her new form. Could anyone's body ever really be theirs when the Message threatened to twist them into something else?

Alto gathered Zelany's still remains against their chest, cradled him to standing, and then nestled him in the cockpit seat, arms curled under his body.

"The only wraith captain in the universe," Alto whispered.

Their remorse felt shallow, less than Zelany deserved, but this was the best Alto could do alone. If they ever made it off this rock, and if they found a genuine wraith specialist, that miracle worker might be able to repair Zelany. New wraith-nodes, new circuits, new tail.

If. The cursed word.

Alto laid a gentle palm on Zelany's nodeless mask. They then plucked up their harmonica and wedged its wooden comb between their left arm's wiry pathways, where it hopefully wouldn't fall out. It was Zelany's only gift that Alto hadn't pried from his body. Carrying it along with the rest only seemed right.

Shuttle readings said the planet offered a warm atmosphere but low oxygen levels. Alto tried donning the spacesuit, but it tore when constricting around the arm-mounted wraith-tail. The helmet only worked in conjunction with the spacesuit, useless now. Alto had to rip out its oxygen bubble pack and stick the black tube in their mouth for air. It tasted of plastic, and its cool flow came laced in chemicals, but the air would see Alto to their destination. They sucked in through their mouth, exhaled through their nose, and then climbed the shuttle's ladder and emerged onto its roof to face this world.

Lumpy maroon slopes climbed from the damp soil in

a vast bowl. Droplets coated the shuttle's roof and the points of its arrow shape, residue of a red-blue mist that wandered the valley. Bodies of water might fill this world. A hopeful crew might have landed their ship here to scout grounds for a future colony.

Alto emerged fully onto the shuttle roof, where a gentle wind coated their skin from head to toe in lukewarm droplets. A light rain landed tinny against Alto's wraith parts. The nakedness didn't bother them, but they wished they had their Yellowjacket coat. Cynical as the reasons might be for Merchant Guild's mascot requirements, Alto would have felt right representing the Yellowjacket's crew and wraiths in the place that had caused their deaths.

Somewhere above this world, the altered crew writhed inside the Yellowjacket's pods. They might have folded into the brain-beast, whoever it used to be, or they might carry on forever as they'd become.

Alto wouldn't know. They were never going back.

The wraith-tail coiled and uncoiled from their right arm, an impatient new limb. If anything like the brain-beast waited ahead, Alto wouldn't be caught unarmed again, and this appendage was stronger than any hammer. Three fingers hung unmoving from their right hand. The wraith-tail must have repurposed those nerves and muscles. Its wires crisscrossed in snaking pathways up Alto's arm, roots for the steel-vertebrae tree.

Alto approached the shuttle's nose and slid to the ground. Their feet smacked soft loam, and they wobbled, nearly fell, righted themselves against the shuttle's hull. After too many crossings stuck in artificial gravity, genuine pressure felt strange on Alto's skin. This world's gravity seemed a hair lighter than E-centric but close enough to go unnoticed after a few steps on its lumpy surface. Alto wished they knew its name.

At least they knew the name of the starship ahead.

It had settled into the crook of the valley, its sides bridging the slopes. Not a lengthy segmented insect, but a comma-shaped single-pod vessel far larger than Pod A of the Yellowjacket. The Star-Hopper seemed a junkheap by starship standards, likely stolen from Merchant Guild by pirates and sold to scrappers on the hunt for salvage.

Traces of Merchant Guild remained—a peaceful green frog sat painted on the hull, its back dotted with black stars. The image faded only at its edges, suggesting touch-ups over time. The new crew must have taken to the frog, wanted to keep him looking sharp. This vessel was personal. They treated it like home, loved it, might even have loved each other.

None of them hailed Alto, as expected. They had come to this planet for their own reasons, and something here had forced them to send the distress call.

Alto sucked air through their tube and crossed the few hundred feet from shuttle to ship. Jagged trails marred the loam, but rainfall had muddied their shapes, distorting any hint as to what might have scraped the soil there. A steel-plated shutter closed the cargo hold, about three feet taller than Alto and maybe ten feet wide. Rain patted the

Star-Hopper's curves. No signs of deterioration; it had not sat here for long. Its painted frog watched blank-eyed from the hull until Alto stepped into the shadow of the ship's underside.

The dirty feeling crossed their mind that this whole incident stemmed from Merchant Guild. Either directly from their devising, or because someone thought the Guild would pay in a big way for whatever might be found here.

Why hadn't the Star-Hopper sent a shuttle down? To land here meant trusting unstable ground with only pronged landing legs, the starship's belly pressed into the planet's surface. It meant wasting fuel to break from this world's gravity. Had the crew found a cargo too large for their shuttle? No way to know from out here, but Alto guessed the Star-Hopper was an all-in-one ship, keeping life support, quarters, cockpit, and cargo hold within a single vessel, like in the pre-wraith days.

And yet a wraith lay coiled on the ground beneath the shuttered entrance.

Alto's steps slowed. A broken wraith had become a bad omen. Only pain followed one's discovery. This wraith looked no different from most—gray husk, steel wraith-plate, the tail, mask, and nodes—but the air tasted worse in Alto's tube the closer they stepped. The wraith's blank black shell weighed heavy with skull and answers.

Alto cradled their oxygen pack under one arm and stroked fingertips down the wraith's mask. Its interface flickered alive, and the light warped where water had settled in a thin sheen. Alto wiped the puddle away; fresh raindrops formed a new one. White-noise fuzz filled the wraith's screen before shifting to dark shapes, and Alto realized what they were watching.

Like the wraith Esme had left in the Yellowjacket's Pod O, there was a video, recorded from this wraith's perspective.

To watch might mean to understand. To know, as the Messenger had suggested. Alto knew of worse fates, likely stemming from whatever this video would show. Better to never watch it, never know a damn thing.

But Alto hadn't come this far to keep themselves in the dark. They hunched over the wraith's upper half, guarded its black mask from further rain, and watched the video play.

17

A face filled the wraith's interface, light skin gone so red and oily with heat and sweat that its odor reached through the screen, same as a bright toothy grin breached a bushy chestnut-going-gray beard. Dark blue eyes gleamed tired yet hopeful. An auburn jacket looked worn and unkempt.

Somewhere behind this visage, a dry nasally voice said, "Watch it, Guy. That's expensive, and you're a man of no means to replace it."

"For now!" Guy guffawed into the screen, fogging it briefly. "But yeah, yeah, got it."

"Not kidding," the phantom voice went on. "Repairs come out of your share."

"Just tinkering," Guy said. His voice was deep but jovial. "We need to record, you know? Posterity-like? When I'm old, I don't know if I'll believe it. Already can't believe it. Can. Not." He glanced over his shoulder, and his shaggy hair parted from the scarred-over crevice of a torn-off ear. "Last chance, Miss Vana. Okay to catch you?"

"I'm not vid-shy," Vana said, same dry tone.

Guy staggered back from the screen, his grin again full of cheery white teeth, and the world opened around him. He stood in a rounded cargo hold, its rust-brown walls curving toward a likewise rusty ceiling maybe ten feet high. Hooks, cords, and stained hammocks held indiscernible lumps overhead. A lanky silhouette crouched atop a tarp-covered curving shape, maybe seven feet long and reaching over Guy's head. A kerchief covered her head, shooting spikes of black hair down her neck. She wore a dark blue jumpsuit and a toolbelt around her waist, while her hands busied with the tarp's cables and cords.

"Here it is," Guy said, gesturing both arms to one side, as if the tarp were anything to present.

Vana peered over the edge. "Just don't say where here is."

"No, no way. This one's ours." Guy strode along the tarp's side and waved to the camera. "Follow me, bud. Get along the front."

Vana scoffed while loosening another tether. "How do we know its front from its back?"

"Same as we know a head from an ass—instinct." Guy laughed himself toward one end of the tarp, nearly tripping over a discarded cord.

Golden light swelled behind him as the video followed with a wraith's smoothness, close to the floor and then rising as it balanced on its unseen tail. The tarp parted in a drooping curtain where the secret underneath arched from its foundation in a hook or claw. Nothing peeked through that shadow, but Guy didn't seem to care. Too busy laughing at his private thoughts. He and Vana already knew what hid beneath the tarp.

"Light but dense," Vana said. "Tough but soft? Not even sure what it's made of." She unhooked another cord, the second to last. Throwing off the tarp would be easy now, but she seemed the meticulous type, never to leave a job almost done. She crept toward the tarp's end.

"Back to Vana," Guy whispered to the screen. He waved a hand, and the wraith's sight followed him down the tarp. "How much you think M-Guild will pay? Sixteen K? Twenty K?"

"That all?" Vana asked, bending over the final cord, a dead snake in her hands. "Better think bigger, or we'll go cross-faction auction."

Guy ran thick chip-nailed fingers through his beard. "Big like that?" His grin was gone; curious puzzlement filled his face.

"It's a first discovery." Vana grunted at the cord. Tied too tight. "Nothing like anyone's seen before. Yeah, that big. Cross-faction, null market. Hell, factionless types too. If a mercenary crew outbids Archons, L.K., M-Guild, why argue? Creds are creds."

"Yeah," Guy said, voice haunted by astonishment.

Joy again filled his beard. "Yeah, yeah, you're right. I'm thinking too small. Everybody'll want this. Why shouldn't we hit it rich?"

Outside the doom of past events, where Alto hunched naked in the rain and vulnerable to the future, a sickness sank in their guts. Their suspicion had been right; the Star-Hopper's crew had found something on this unknown world worth a hefty price, at least to them, and expected Merchant Guild or someone else to pay in a big way. Maybe Guy, Vana, Captain Afsar Sajid, and the rest of the Star-Hopper's crew had dreams, or debts like Alto's, or both. Every side of civilization squeezed until the desperate turned to extremes, like this tarp and its secret.

What had this ship of scrappers found?

"All factions, give your bid," Guy said, clapping his hands three times as if prompting the ceiling to rain money. His laughter echoed through the Star-Hopper's cargo hold. "Even Luminous Kingdom would take a shot, if only to destroy it and say it never existed."

"That bother you?" Vana asked. Her hands at last unknotted the final cord, and it slithered down the tarp's side.

"No way; like you said, creds are creds. And fame's fame. We're famous, you know that?" Guy's face again filled the screen. "I'm famous. Can you believe it?" He veered back to Vana, looming over him. "Wait until Janey hears. Papa left home a scrapper, came back famous."

Vana folded the tarp against itself on the far side,

away from the video's view. Any minute now, the secret would bare itself to the screen. "Kids don't care if their parents are famous," she said. "You'll be her Papa forever. Nothing more."

Guy held still, digesting these words, and then let out a mirthful sigh. "Well, that's not so bad either."

Vana tensed her shoulders, as if about to peel the tarp away in one firm thrust, and then her body jerked to her left. She swatted at empty air, and then again at a cord hanging from the ceiling. A shrill cry leaped up her throat.

"Vana?" Guy called.

"What's in here?" Vana asked, standing. She paced the tarp's curtain-like front, where the secret beneath pointed deeper into the ship. "Who's creeping around? Captain? Talia? Or Mo, is that you?"

Nothing changed in the video's quality, its picture murky and walls firm, and yet Alto's heart sank. If only the wraith could have seen through human eyes, it might have captured a purple-tinted world of contorting shapes and memories. Alto couldn't guess what might live inside this recorded moment. They only knew it had found the scrappers' minds.

Guy gaped at the floor and then fell to his knees. "Janey? Janey, what—how—what's wrong? Janey!"

He cradled an unseen load in one hand the way he might hold a child's head, while his other hand scooped at the floor. Was he burying his Janey, or piling her guts into her torso? His sudden sobs could mean either. Likely a violet sheen coated her skin.

Vana groped at the ceiling and yanked a bulky chain free from its hook. "I want to know who's in here right now!" she screamed.

The mind-hack seemed to be sparing her the worst. Credit to some unseen augmentation, maybe, but without a wraith-node planted in her head, and a wire already in her brain to tether and survive it, she could only stall the inevitable.

Alto watched both Star-Hopper crewmates thrash at thin air, caught in a broken wraith's interface and the unchangeable past. Not that Alto could have helped had they been there. They would have only watched, same as they'd watched Esme, the way they'd slept through every flesh-hack down the Yellowjacket. What had Alto been doing when the Star-Hopper's crew met their fate? Giving Yellowjacket comms a maintenance check? Chatting with Esme? Fucking her? Innocent moments, never to return.

In the doomed video, Guy and Vana gave up fighting the air to instead fight at themselves, striking their abdomens and skulls, their foreheads banging and banging on any surface they could find until each collapsed in a throbbing heap. Their backs bubbled into lopsided hills. Shabby clothing and dull jumpsuit stretched and shredded from the rising mounds, skin sloughing from muscle, muscle sliding from cracking bones. Faces and limbs seemed to cave in on themselves, drained and then folding. The new forms needed greater mass, more tissue, their shapes rewritten by an unseen hand upon the surface of human flesh.

Wrinkled forms of swollen brains emerged from each sinewy cocoon. Tubes tore at Guy's deflated sides and pulled the chest-sized brain free from his ravaged back. Above him, the once-Vana brain squirmed toward the tarp's edge and slid to the floor. The tarp wrinkled behind and then began to slide after her.

The video caught the briefest flash of a black shape wreathed in purple light—not something Alto recognized as tech by Merchant Guild, Archons, or any other known faction—before the point of view veered toward the floor.

Guy's brain form had tugged the wraith's tail out from under its torso. Writhing tubes climbed its wraith-plate and filled its screen with a faceless wrinkled lump. The video stilled, as if Guy's beard might sprout down the brain and return his grin, showing he remembered being human.

The video then swerved from the brain and thrust at the dirty floor. And reeled back. And thrust again. Back again. Thrust into blackness. Stayed there.

Alto let the rain slide into their eyes, down their nose. It was a reminder of the world outside the video, and yet what they'd seen had reached beyond the wraith's interface, the planet's atmosphere, into the Yellowjacket. Into another starship, and more, and how far would it go?

A dark curving shape had peeked beneath Vana's tarp at the last moment. Clarity eluded the wraith's video, but Alto had a feeling if they stepped inside the Star-Hopper, they would get a better look than they really wanted.

There was nowhere else to go.

Alto set the wraith's head on the ground, as gentle as when they'd set Zelany in his seat, and then stood and faced the Star-Hopper's underside. Doubtful Guy or Vana had locked its shutter after hauling in their mysterious cargo or sealed its inside for takeoff into space. They hadn't been ready to leave yet and had no reason to expect anyone else would visit this miserable planet. Alto only needed to heave the shutter open. They might find the cargo hold from the video. They might find worse.

Alto grasped a handle, their left arm tensing with circuits and muscle, and slid the shutter up into the Star-Hopper's hull. The weight sank against their fingers. It would not hold open on its own, Alto realized, and the windy pressure against their face suggested the ship's air system hadn't yet quit. They stepped inside and let steel crash behind them. They then spat out their air tube, shut the oxygen pack's valve, and laid it against the shutter in case they would need it again in leaving.

But they doubted it.

Steel fragments dotted the floor where Guy's feral brain must have dragged the broken wraith outside. Alto stared down at one slender vertebra, blinked several times to let their eyes adjust, and then looked again into the starship's depths.

The cargo hold stretched wider than shown in the video. Something had torn out the starship walls, the once-rusty ceiling, hollowing the Star-Hopper into one enormous space.

Not an unfamiliar one. Alto had seen it veiled in purple when cleaving feral brains' minds, its walls painted red and black, floor decorated in organs, sticky pools, and bits of bone, as if someone had run out of starship parts and decided to remake the cargo hold with human flesh.

The cathedral of gore. And what awaited at its center.

18

Frail golden light leaked from the cracked-open cockpit on the far side of the open space, some fragment of power still lighting the Star-Hopper. Its weakness gave depth to shadows across the hollowed starship's constructed innards, now coated by innards of the human kind. The surface seemed to move whenever Alto blinked, but that might have been the light playing tricks on their eyes, worn out after all the running and crying and misery.

They recognized what stood at the cathedral's center. Its form was unprecedented, at least by human experience, but its function stood obvious to a communications specialist. Alto's training had meant learning everything from the most modern forms of digital signature to the ancient radios of old Earth. You never knew what kind of slapped-together junk someone might use on some backwater moon, and they would need their hired communications specialist to both understand and repair or improve it.

Antennas were rare anymore. Alto had seen pictures of them jutting from historic vehicles, video boxes, antique handheld comms. And Alto had seen insects.

The Star-Hopper could already speak across space. Its comms station would resemble most others in Merchant Guild ships, current and former. Captain Sajid's distress call had reached beyond the planet by design.

But the feral brains had no use or understanding for A.I., wraiths, computers, reason enough to destroy them so thoroughly. No longer human, therefore no longer compatible with human machines. And without computers, the brains had lacked the means to spread what they really wanted to say through the Star-Hopper's comms station, so they built their own means, an antenna they could operate and understand.

Using their own bodies.

Black wires snaked from the walls and met in the cathedral's center, their ends driven into the wrinkled mass of an enormous pink-gray brain. Bigger than Alto, bigger than their room on the Yellowjacket. A deep ravine carved through its center. Its sides swelled and deflated in a gentle rhythm, as if it somehow breathed.

Beneath its dripping underside, a black shape formed a half crescent at the cathedral's center, striped with pulsating violet light. A wet sheen coated its surface. There was something earthen about it, like rock and soil, and yet made of living or once-living tissue, some insectile carapace or bone or the husk of a cocoon, all cobbled together and then left to the elements. Unknowing scrappers had dragged it to the Star-Hopper sometime later, where it joined their new humans-turned-grand brain form to become a strange altar of mind.

And not for this place alone. The altar was the antenna's shaft; the grand brain was its peak, powerful enough to launch signals from the planet's surface and into immediate space. The distress call lured starships into range with benign words—*Captain Afsar Sajid of the Star-Hopper. Only a handful of us left now, and we need immediate extraction from planet's surface. Please help, anyone*—but this antenna said something else. It would enter secretly into nearby minds, the same psionic virus as had infected the Star-Hopper crew, now reaching for anyone who dared approach this world to help.

The Message.

"You will not need me for much longer," a gentle voice said.

The Messenger crawled from behind the altar of mind and mounted the grand brain. Its form flitted like a violet dancer around the hanging wires driven into the brain's craggy surface and then paused at the wrinkled front to stare with glowing eyes.

No more blur or shadow or clouds or light. Aside from the violet sheen, the Messenger looked like Alto from before they began sticking wraith parts into their body.

"Once the Message is known, there is no need for the

170

Messenger." An arm cast ceilingward as the Messenger craned its head back. "You will know as the others have known, and I will find new recipients to spread the Message."

Alto stepped deeper into the cathedral. The floor was as warm as Esme's skin used to be. To keep going would mean treading in the still-living tissue of the Star-Hopper's crew. Their discovery gleamed purple at the altar of mind, as if it knew the revulsion of this touch and delighted in it.

"They found it, or dug it up, huh?" Alto asked. "Hauled it here, where it started to change them. The captain put out her call for help, and then that thing turned the crew into this." They gestured a circuit-coated hand toward the monstrous brain. "And it reached out for us and started to change us, too."

"It is the Message," the Messenger said. "It is one with me."

Alto took another warm step into the cathedral. "You're not it," they said, nodding first to the altar of mind and then to the grand brain. "You're them. The crew, passing along what hurt them."

"Is that not what I've told you? It is the womb from which I am birthed, the shadowless dark, the place unblemished by starlight. I am the Messenger, as all I have ever said." The Messenger lowered its reverent arm and gestured down at the brain, beneath the brain, to the purple-black altar. "Carrying the Message."

"Whose—" Alto faltered at their next step, something

171

wet gushing between their toes. No looking down; only looking to the light of the pulsating altar. "Whose is it? Where's it come from?"

"It comes from the dark. The outer dark." The Messenger's peaceful expression faded into a mild scowl. "Outer. Out."

Alto stepped again, ten paces from the altar's foundation. "Do you know?"

"Through the dark. Outer dark. Outside the universe. Outside." The Messenger's confidence returned, and its eyes glowed at Alto. "Outsiders. Beyond us."

"You don't have the words, do you?" Alto asked. Nine steps away.

"Neither do you," the Messenger said. "Your limits are mine. My intent breathes from this place and the dark and the everywhere, but how you see me is your fault." Its head cocked to one side. "Like so many things."

The grand brain trembled beneath the Messenger's feet. A purple cloud slid across Alto's eyes—

Esme's husk, scalp and skin dribbling, bone cage shattered from organs, a dark lump rising, slathered in entrails, Zelany curled, needful, helpless.

—and then dissipated.

Alto covered their gaping mouth in horror. Esme might not stay a small feral brain writhing between pods forever. She might join the brain-beast, and it might mold her and everyone else into another grand brain. The Yellowjacket would become a new antenna, one circling this world and broadcasting the Message even deeper into space. Never as intense as here in the altar's presence, but powerful enough to hack distant minds, distant flesh.

The Messenger crouched at the grand brain's edge, knees around its head, face leering toward Alto. "You walk the edge of understanding. You are so close to giving in. Tear off these nodes and plates and circuits and tail. Free your flesh. Welcome me through these crude machines, into you. Know the Message."

Alto took a deep breath. The cathedral of gore did not smell of rotting flesh or coppery blood. It smelled of human odor, skin and sweat. And a sweetness, too.

It smelled something like Esme.

"If I let you in—" Alto's voice cracked at their next step. "If I do, I'll know the Message, right?"

"You will," the Messenger said, leaning deeper over the grand brain's front. "At last."

"And what happens when I know the Message?" Alto asked.

The Messenger pursed its lips.

Alto glanced to the skin-painted walls, the webbed tubes that might have once been intestines, the wires coursing down into the altar of mind, crowned with the grand brain. All parts of people who'd met their own versions of the Messenger, be they kind or cruel or shapeless. They had come to know the same unifying Message written in their flesh.

"No," Alto said. One hand gestured down their body, and they stood tall amid the cathedral of gore. "This much is mine. I don't want to know your Message, and I don't want it to take what belongs to me and no one else. I want none of this shit to have ever happened, but since I can't do that, I want it to stop." One foot edged forward. "It's going to stop."

"The Message is endless," the Messenger said, sneering. "It has been waiting in the dark for discovery. It will wait long after you have gone."

Alto tensed their body fist-tight and stormed the altar, feet kicking at fragments of bone, a wire snapping under heel, Zelany's wraith-tail coiling and uncoiling from their right arm like a clenching fist. They were done with this. All of it. Message, Messenger, mind-hack, flesh-hack, everything.

Enough.

"The Message could be yours," the Messenger said. "But you choose death."

The cathedral clouded beneath a bruised mountain of inner snow. Bitter cold stabbed tiny icicles across Alto's skin, even where the wraith-plate hugged their torso. All in their head, and yet real in its own way. Voices howled in the blizzard's wind.

"She never liked you," the Messenger said, dancing somewhere in the gale. "Bored woman. Idle Alto." A thin hand clawed at Alto's left arm, its fingers scraping above the place where Alto had hooked their harmonica. "Zelany was loyal and showed you so. Programmed that way. Trapped under the personality you chose, his insights and assistance hampered by your need for entertainment. Bored Alto, using Zelany. Bored Esme, using Alto."

"Is that the Message?" Alto snapped. "Is that all it has to say?" They were five paces from the altar of mind. Bone shrapnel bit at their heels.

"The Message is not told," the Messenger said. "It is only known."

Alto bared their teeth to one side. "And you don't know it, do you?"

An impatient breath hissed in Alto's ear. Flesh stretched like tearing paper across the cathedral's rim, where it bubbled with maroon forms rising into Alto-high pillars. Limbs split from figures' sides, dripping sticky red ringlets, and hooks of bone emerged in their lumpy hands.

Echoes of the surgeons in past mind-hacks. Were these new mind-hacks, too, or were they flesh-hacks? Harmless figments or genuine threats?

"It all hurts," the Messenger said, its voice adrift in the violet snowstorm. "It is all real, one way or another."

Alto tore their attention back to the altar of mind. If they acted fast, they wouldn't think, and if they didn't think, they wouldn't overthink into doing nothing. Letting the bad side of their brain have a say had never helped them. Their arms and legs would do the thinking now, along with Zelany's wraith-tail, and Alto's teeth, and a deep rage they hadn't known before this disaster began.

"There's a little vengeance in you, huh?" a familiar voice asked.

Alto wheeled to one side, and their right arm lifted the wraith-tail.

Esme stepped at Alto's left, violet eyes alight. "Only caught a glimpse of it in your sessions." Her smile shined brighter through the blizzard than the golden light at the cathedral's back. "It was almost like under the bad thoughts, you were mad at yourself for having them. You should be. Deep down, they're your fault. The brain is to blame, but it's your brain. Part of that body you love so much."

Alto eyed the altar and then Esme. "You're not real."

"Are you sure?" Esme asked. Far behind her, hook-wielding figures staggered closer. "You've thought that before." Her hand traced Alto's clavicle, their dark nipple, their wraith-plate. "And you were wrong. Remember what you did to me when you were wrong?"

Alto's right arm tensed overhead. Wouldn't lower to their side. Wouldn't strike Esme down and dispel the illusion, either.

"They put me back together the way you wanted." Esme pressed close. Was she clothed or naked? Alto couldn't tell through the thickening psionic snowstorm, but her skin felt warm, and she breathed sweet air. "The world of flesh is like words to the outsiders. They rewrote me wrong before, so they wiped it away and wrote me again the way I used to be. For you."

The surgeons drew closer, but Alto couldn't distinguish each from the falling snow. Purple clouds filled their head with Esme's sloughing skin, snapping bones, and the dark lump of brain emerging from her back.

An Esme-like hand touched Alto's face. "What if my transformation was the illusion? The violet in my eyes then would've been the mind-hack, and you can't tell the difference anymore. It's a violet, violent world. You might be lying in the Yellowjacket, passed out from your spacewalk, or from fucking me, or you've just driven yourself into a blackout with bad thoughts. All your dreams are sound and color. How would you know the difference?"

Alto breathed deep again. Could a scent be purple? No idea, but Esme couldn't know Alto dreamed in the abstract.

Not a mistakenly false Esme, but a true illusion.

Alto lowered their arm and leaned close as if to kiss, another apology on their lips. "Forgive me." Their breath seeped against a face bright with violet eyes.

The false Esme burst into snow and nothingness, and the surgeons fluttered into wind behind her. No look of pain on her face. She'd been nothing but the Messenger's tool. Not Esme. Not anything that could forgive Alto.

But her words were true—Alto was to blame. The problem was in their head, the way they saw the Messenger, the way they'd struck out with a mind as sharp as a blade to pierce the small brain-beast on the Yellowjacket and caught this terrible psionic virus.

If they could throw a psionic assault outward, they could turn another inward. A mind-hack of the self-inflicted kind.

Somewhere within the purple blizzard, the Messenger's Alto-like form strode nearer, its narrow form dipping and dancing out of winding shadows. Ready for anything, it probably believed.

Alto tensed their thoughts, and their forehead glowed with wraith-nodes, but instead of pressing the purple mirage out, Alto drew inward. Deeper, sleeker, not quite a mind-sword, more a mind-sword's sheathe. Its crevice grew arms and legs and face. The form ached in Alto's heart, weighted by guilt, but they needed to fill it with humanity or else there was no hope.

The new figure drifted from Alto's thoughts and through the psionic blizzard, her violet eyes aiming for the Messenger.

Another Esme.

The Messenger froze in place, its dance caught in ice. Maybe it thought the grand brain had dredged this Esme up without the Messenger's knowing. Its face became dull and unreadable.

Esme's smile was a sunrise breaching the snowstorm. She approached the Messenger and raised one hand, fingers curled around a purple-rimmed likeness of Alto's harmonica.

"Play for me," Esme said.

The Messenger turned its placid face to Alto. "Do not mistake me for you," it said. "Do not assume your weakness lives in me."

Alto tensed their thoughts again, firm yet gentle.

Like Esme. "You're another idea from the bad side of Alto's brain," she said. "The snow before clear weather."

"I am the Messenger. I am the dark, and the dark is—" The Messenger's face twitched into a toothy sneer. It rattled back and forth as if to shake Esme away and then flashed a perplexed stare toward Alto. "You have made a strange and convincing intrusion."

Alto breathed deep and focused. One foot forward. Another thought deep. They needed to reach the bottom of their heart for this to work.

The Messenger only knew Esme through the distorted veil of Alto's anxious inner snow. It had never known the real woman. Even Alto could only project their best impression, but that was closer to her elusive truth than the bad side of their brain had ever cobbled together from paranoid doubts and unfair misperceptions. Alto had glances and conversations, memories and touch. It wasn't much, they and Esme hadn't known each other well, but a chance meeting and parting from a wonderful mind was better than never crossing her path at all.

Esme reached for the Messenger's shoulder. "Do you still want this?" She slid closer, its face nearing hers. "That's all that matters."

The Messenger's back straightened, and its calm melted away. "Only the Message matters. You're a desperate idea from an ignorant mind."

But it believed in her, or else it wouldn't talk to her. Even the grand brain's mind could be hacked.

The Messenger pressed a step into Esme. "I am only

the dark, filtered into Alto. And you are a regret given form. You cannot hurt me." It flung a violet arm, eager to dispel her. Watching her burst into snowflakes would hurt Alto more than the Messenger, the only reason it had let her illusion vanish before.

But Alto had no intention of letting their false Esme go. The Messenger pressed through her.

And fell into her.

Arms spread wide from her body and split from palms to elbows in a nest of writhing tubes, their edges lined with metal teeth. Each new limb coiled around the Messenger's trunk, its arms, its neck. It jerked back, flung an arm forward, and fell deeper into her bodily snare.

At the room's center, the grand brain recoiled.

"You cannot keep me," the Messenger said. It turned again to Alto, tugging desperately at every limb, but Esme's barbed coils held. "I am everywhere."

"But I'm not like other therapists," Esme said, grasping the messenger's jaw and yanking its face toward her smile. "I must've said it over and over, right? I'm a fun therapist."

Alto watched them a moment, the struggle playing out in the cathedral as much as in their head. If the Messenger wanted Alto's mindscape so badly, it could enjoy the barbed-wire twist of their personal joy. They turned to the grand brain and took another step. Four paces away.

The Messenger reeled. "You killed her, so don't pretend otherwise. She is gone."

The brain's front lobe loomed over the purple altar's crescent. Three paces.

The Messenger writhed, but Esme's barbed-wire body flowed in a brain-beastly flood. If the Messenger broke this illusion with its own mind-sword, would the false Esme dig inside the grand brain? Or would Alto find a psionic doorway and step through?

Two paces away.

Snowfall thinned, the grand brain's mind-hack weakening, but a new pressure clutched at Alto's muscles. The air hung tight around the altar, its gravity cranked up high over E-centric. It pressed with mind-hack, flesh-hack, the work of the mysterious outsiders insisting their Message reach inside Alto's body.

Alto could do one better. Climbing up to the grand brain meant scaling the altar, skin to whatever substance formed its surface. It wanted this touch? Alto would give it.

They reached out their right hand and pressed limp fingers into the altar's soft-yet-hard surface.

Icy pinpricks jabbed down Alto's arm, a flood of tingling screams. Shadows clawed at mind's edge. An unseen fist squeezed Alto's body, and fresh static mimicked a poor signal between two starships, some communication's meaning lost between language, structure, and a distance Alto couldn't comprehend. Their wraith pieces guarded mind and flesh from hacking, but as Alto pushed into the altar, the static only deepened.

Oh yes. The nightmare made some sense now. It was

cruel, and wrong, and a mistake, but the rushing noise inside Alto didn't lie.

Their body and mind could not understand because there could be no understanding. There was no part of the Message the human mind could process. No interface for human physiology. No alien bodies, and so no compatibility between non-terrestrial biology and the people of the Star-Hopper, Yellowjacket, or the unfortunate other starship to follow the Messenger's lure.

But this was the difference between thoughts and non-thoughts. When two people spoke different languages or through text or hand gesture, they used means the other might access. Independent ideas followed similar human interfaces.

There was no interface for the body itself beneath the Message, and neither was there an interface for the human mind. Only noise and impulses and consequence carried through this psionic webbing, the Message eager to write itself across the only medium it understood—flesh.

Alto began to laugh, an aching wet rhythm in their throat.

There had never been any sinister psionic underbelly reaching from the Star-Hopper into the Yellowjacket, no infection by an alien virus. Not even thoughts. Every broken wraith, every ended life, every awful moment of gut-wrenching screaming pain came down to the simple incompatible pulsation between minds.

Alto collapsed against the fragment, aching with laughter, as if their noise might undo this cosmic misunderstanding, but its nonsensical psionic output did not waver at their fingertips or their cackling. It had no ears to hear, no nerves to feel. Humans lived in bodies and cast out their thoughts in speech and words and gesture. The outsiders could be thoughts, and they cast out their intentions in bodies and flesh. Whatever biological receptor might have interpreted the altar's Message, Alto was lacking. All humans were, yet they had taken this discovery as if everything encountered through the vastness of space were meant for mankind.

Wrong, all wrong. The fragment's psionic signal was an expression unread. No matter the human desperation to carry out some jumbled order from within to spread the Message, it would only emerge as noise and nonsense. Every attempt to obey could only lead to suffering and madness.

A miscommunication in the stars, nothing more.

Alto stood trembling and swallowed another laugh before it could crack into a sob. Their grasping hands hauled their body up the altar's side, its surface crackling with stone and carapace until Alto reached the grand brain.

The Messenger had quit fighting below. It now trembled on its knees beneath the false Esme's grasp, as if teetering somewhere between mercy and surrender.

"They speak through the flesh-hack, but that isn't how we listen," Alto said. "You carried a Message you didn't understand. Could never understand." They laid one palm against the grand brain and let its throbbing warmth seep through their skin. "There was never anything to know."

The Messenger craned its neck. "There is the dark."

Alto drew their hand back. "I know the dark. It's a friendlier place than you think, full of stars and planets and people. And no matter how awful they might turn out to be sometimes, they don't deserve their bodies being used as paper to write some outsider's Message. Even if that's your only purpose."

The wraith-tail uncoiled down Alto's arm. Wraiths were harmless, programmed to be that way. Their parts were not.

Alto was not.

They raised their right arm high overhead and then lashed the tail whiplike across the grand brain's side, cutting steel vertebral spines in a ragged gash. Tissue rippled across hills of pink-gray flesh, and a slit of red ichor spat warmth over Alto's legs.

"Another mistake, another Perfect Alto Fuck-Up," the Messenger said, a desperation in its voice. "Your bad habit. You'll kill the way to knowing."

"There's nothing to know," Alto said, heaving now. "What the Message does—it happened to these people for nothing. They did it to us for nothing!"

Alto reeled back again and cut the wraith-tail through another stretch of pink-gray flesh. Thick dark blood splashed their face and chest, coating skin and steel, but Alto slashed again, eager for the crimson rain.

This was not an ordinary brain. It jerked and spasmed with nerves, and misty breath quickened in and out.

Likely every feral brain had needed to form new anatomy inside. The Message had only changed them into the shape it might have thought best told its meaning, but a creature still needed basic functions to live. Severing those functions would let it die.

Alto glanced at the black wires stretching from every side of the cathedral of gore and then whipped the wraith-tail across the nearest one.

It snapped from the brain in a spray of red-and-black fluid. Not a wire, but a tube pouring—what? Blood? Engine leakage? Alto didn't know. Whatever the substance, the grand brain would never taste another drop. Alto clambered up the brain's spongy surface, fresh blood clinging to their skin, and slashed at another tube.

The Messenger seemed to stretch from the false Esme's grasp. "But the Message!"

"There's no Message for us, don't you get that?" Alto asked, breath hissing through their teeth. "Whatever they want to tell us, we can't understand it. All it does is kill who we are. You don't know it because you can't. Never been alive. You're a bad dream, and I'm stopping the dreamers."

The Messenger went quiet, as if trying to find words for its Message. It knew nothing. It could only grab the Message from the altar and carry it, a sealed file to be read by no one, poisoning everyone who dared look. Alto had only been spared because pieces of the dead protected them. Esme's help. Parts of wraith. These had guarded Alto against this nightmare.

Alto would do right by them. The wraith-tail—*Zelany's* wraith-tail—stiffened and cut another tube.

The Messenger twitched again. "But I am the Messenger," it pleaded.

"And I—" Alto began. They cut the last tube and dredged the words from deep inside. "I am the truth behind the universe!" The wraith-tail carved a deep chasm in the grand brain's frontal lobe.

The Messenger recoiled; its violet eyes stretched wide.

Alto thrashed again. "From which inspiration mankind sowed the seeds of torment!"

"You cannot end me," the Messenger said. "It is wrong to end me."

Alto whipped again, and again, brain bits flying, blood spraying. "In the fertile perceptions of their terrible minds!"

Shimmering tears coated the Messenger's face. "But what about the Message?"

Alto's arm was growing heavy. They beat again. They couldn't stop. "Now nurtured and grown into nightmare thoughts." Panting, exhausted, but they had to finish this.

"I want to live," the Messenger said.

Fragments split from its face in a puff of violet snow and then reformed into Esme-like cheeks, rosy and full of life. Her voice spilled from shifting lips in a forlorn moan like Alto had never heard, but real. Too real.

"I want to live too," the Esme-faced Messenger said. "Why won't you let me live?"

Alto shut their eyes and tensed their tired arm. This wasn't Esme. She was gone and never coming back.

Zelany's wraith-tail stiffened straight from Alto's forearm, a spike to echo the mind-blade, and they aimed at the flesh beneath their feet. The grand brain was to blame. Now it would stop.

"Within the mindscape of emptiness, endlessness, and death," Alto said.

They reeled their arm back and drove the wraith-tail through the grand brain's center, puncturing its surface, its depths, down and down until steel vertebrae clanged against the altar below.

Tendons snapped inside. Unseen lungs sighed a steaming cloud as the fleshy mound sagged. Purple veins mapped the air, the cathedral of gore, the living tissue writhing in one gargantuan psionic scream.

Alto grasped their head, screaming with it. Thoughts so violet, and thoughts so violent, crashing, biting, clawing, a desperation to spread a misunderstood word into the universe. An unknowable death speech with no one to hear it.

And then the purple snapped away, and Alto collapsed.

The grand brain sloughed to each side of the altar, impermeant in its death. Flesh melted down the cathedral. Whatever tensed muscle had kept the human remains spread across these walls now shriveled to nothing, its energy gone. The altar dripped on all sides with an organic puddle the way a heated page might bleed with ink.

Alto staggered to their feet and looked around. This was no cathedral of any kind. It was only the insides of a battered starship once piloted by the unluckiest people who'd ever drifted into space.

The last remnants of the Messenger shattered, a cloud of inner snow melting into shadows and then air. The false Esme faded beside it. Alto had quit tensing their thoughts, and the illusion drifted like an old memory, its details lost and leaving only scars behind.

The mindscape lay empty as if cleansed.

Alto stood unmoving atop the limp brain, listening for some sign of life. Their own breath slid in and out, no other, and blood dripped down their skin and wraith-plate. They drew the rigid tail up from the grand brain, let it curl against their arm again, and slid to the fleshy floor beside the altar of mind. Soon this space would reek of decay. That seemed only right.

Static echoed off starship walls, chased by a gravelly voice. "Star-Hopper, come in. This is Comms Specialist Meia of the Archon Triumph."

Alto turned toward the golden light sneaking through a crack in the wall from the Star-Hopper's cockpit. Archon Triumph? Alto remembered that ship from a long-gone war they'd never been part of. Archons fighting Luminous Kingdom. Studied by Merchant Guild. Years had passed, and vast stretches of space, but now this ship had arrived here, same as Alto.

Lured by a distress call.

Archons might be safer than Merchant Guild for an extraction; they would have no use for Alto's body full of wraith parts, but the Triumph was a warship without a war. What would its crew of soldiers make of the former cathedral of gore? How close would they step to the altar's field of influence?

"Hang tight, we're sending a shuttle," Meia went on. "If you can, state the nature of your emergency so we'll be best prepared."

A fist of air pressed at Alto's back, and they turned to face the altar.

Without the grand brain to amplify its signal, no Message would carve through space and speak itself into starship crew bodies. Still the Message lingered here in its purest form, as the Star-Hopper crew had found it on this sad little world. Trapped here, as before. Alto had no idea how or why the crew had come and found it, and guessed no one would ever know.

But they knew why the M.G. Yellowjacket had come, and the Merchant Guild ship with the squid mascot, and now the Archon Triumph. Even if Alto left the Star-Hopper and hailed the Archon shuttle from afar, one or more of them would see the Star-Hopper and grow curious. No guarantee they'd believe Alto on why it was best to let that curiosity die on this world with the Star-Hopper's crew. The Archons would want to see for themselves.

They would know the Message, and the Message would know them in return, and the nightmare would start all over again.

Alto could kill the Star-Hopper's comms, let the Archons lose this ship's location.

Or Alto could kill the Message.

The altar's black-and-purple surface shimmered expectantly. How to begin dismantling it? Killing it? Alto wasn't sure it could be destroyed by their means at hand. Its age hid outside human knowledge and comprehension, same as the outsiders who'd built it, or birthed it, or spat it up and forgotten about it, oblivious to the hell it would someday unleash.

No, Alto doubted the outsiders had forgotten. They had left the Message here to be found, maybe by humans, maybe by something else long extinct. Its surface grasped at the air, wanting, needing. If the outsiders were thoughts, and bodies were their speech, while humans were bodily forms and gave their thoughts speech, then the Message would remain forever unknown, only readable as pointless carnage.

Could the reverse be done to the outsiders? If they were thoughts, then would Alto's psionics malform the outsiders' existence the way their Message had malformed human bodies?

Alto pressed a hand to the altar's hard surface again and tensed their mind.

They weren't sure how to begin. A threat? A mind-hack? What was the outsiders' nature? In the end, they might have never meant to hurt anyone. They might have only wanted to communicate, oblivious to the trouble that their minds were not compatible with all receivers. Thoughts written in meat versus meat writing its thoughts. It was everyone's fault, and no one's.

The longer Alto touched the altar, the deeper its insides rang against their palm, like an echo through an underground cavern. This was not an object seated here, but a window with dirty glass, a passageway caught in an old snapshot suggesting time, place, and depth untouchable from this side of its carapace, as if the universe awaited within.

The body of the altar was the Message. And like most messages, it awaited a reply.

Alto couldn't speak in ways it would understand, and its flesh-twisting language couldn't cross Alto's bodily machines, but maybe something else could link them. Some way to tell the outsiders to stop. To give communication was not an empty gesture, even if the receiver couldn't understand, for better or worse or nothing at all.

Static again echoed through the Star-Hopper ahead of word from the Archons. "Hang tight," Meia said again. "Med crew's coming. Ten clicks or less."

Not much time. Alto reached into the crook of their left arm and plucked their harmonica from the nest of wires and circuits. How much music could anyone play in ten clicks? Hopefully enough to matter, if this gambit had the slightest chance of ending the nightmare once and for all.

Alto nestled into the altar's foundation, their spine

planted against its strange soft-hard surface. They then lifted the harmonica, pressed its brass reed plates against their lips, and tried to relax their mind. The air tensed with breath and then eased with it. The world purpled as Alto reached a crackling thought outward in hopes that somehow this fragment of human willpower would pierce the altar's inner universe.

It would be a new Message like the outsiders on the far end of this connection had never known. With any luck, the kind of Message that would hurt no one.

Alto let their mindscape spread, closed their eyes, and began to play a nameless song.

Afterword

Most of my books begin with ideas and characters occurring to me in snippets and then merging together over time until I realize I have notes for a book on my hands. *Your Mind Is a Terrible Thing* the novella began with Samantha Kolesnik telling me, "You should write a space horror book."

At first, I kind of laughed it off. When would I have time? How could I come up with something just like that?

But then I thought about it for a minute and went, "Well, *if* I were to write one, I'd want some cyberpunk in there, and psychic stuff, and spacewalks" and so on, and within an hour I found myself furiously scribbling notes for characters, scenes, and a world. Those notes eventually became an outline, which mutated several times before I started the book, and that changed several times as I wrote and revised.

I say all this to point out that this novella was not in my plans, but it grew into existence anyway. We can't dictate what we'll make, especially when friends plant seeds in our heads. In the end, what came out of that suggestion was a far more personal book than I expected in many ways. I'm so grateful to Sam for that, and for hearing me out as I worked on what ended up being a lonely yet frantic project.

I also want to thank Cooper, Cassie, and Becca of the PikeCast for the influence their discussions had in elements of this book. If pressed, I couldn't specify exactly which layers are me and which are bits of freewheeling chaos from listening to their talks, but I felt that Anything Goes magic as I developed and wrote this spacey strangeness.

I'm grateful to Waylon for taking on an odd project of this kind. It can be a difficult road into the stars.

And eternal thanks to my wife J for her galaxy's worth of support, patience, and love.

About the Author

Hailey Piper is the author of *The Worm and His Kings*, also from Off Limits Press, as well as horror novellas *Benny Rose the Cannibal King* and *The Possession of Natalie Glasgow*, short story collection *Unfortunate Elements of My Anatomy*, and horror novel *Queen of Teeth*. She is an active member of the Horror Writers Association, with over seventy short stories appearing in *Pseudopod*, *Vastarien*, *Year's Best Hardcore Horror*, *Daily Science Fiction*, *Dark Matter Magazine*, *Cast of Wonders*, *Flash Fiction Online*, *The Arcanist*, and other publications. A trans woman hailing from the haunted woods of New York, she now lives with her wife in Maryland, where their paranormal research is classified.

Find Hailey at www.haileypiper.com or on Twitter via @HaileyPiperSays.

Printed in the USA
CPSIA information can be obtained
at www.ICGtesting.com
LVHW011057250124
769695LV00004B/302

9 781737 463351